SECRETS OF A
MOONLIT RIVER

SECRETS OF A
MOONLIT RIVER

BRENDAN GRIFFIN

Red Hen Publishing

First published in 2013 by
Red Hen Publishing
Duagh, Listowel, Co. Kerry, Ireland
Tel: 00353 68 45942
www.redhenpublishing.ie
redhen1@eircom.net

ISBN: 978-0-9927487-0-8

Typesetting and design by Fairways Design
www.fairwaysdesign.com

Printed and bound by Walsh Colour Print, Tralee Road, Castleisland, Co. Kerry, Ireland.

This book may be purchased online at
www.brendangriffinbooks.com

© Brendan Griffin 2013

All rights reserved. No part of this publication may be reproduced or used in any form or by any means – photographic, electronic or mechanical, including photocopying, recording, taping or information storage and retrieval systems – without the prior permission of the copyright owner in writing.

A CIP catalogue record for this book is available from the British Library.

For Róisín and Micheál

CONTENTS

Foreword	ix
CHAPTER ONE	1
CHAPTER TWO	31
CHAPTER THREE	49
CHAPTER FOUR	71
CHAPTER FIVE	89
CHAPTER SIX	100
CHAPTER SEVEN	127
EPILOGUE	142

FOREWORD

An empty rural pub, late on a weeknight in the depth of winter, can be an inspiring place. In 2007, I made the decision to renovate an old pub in the village of Castlemaine, County Kerry, which I subsequently ran for three years with my then girlfriend, Róisín, who would become my wife in 2009. It was there in the Castle Inn, usually after closing the bar and cleaning up on the quiet week nights, that I first started working on what would - ultimately - become *Secrets of a Moonlit River*, often writing until the small hours of the morning outside the bar counter.

With the glowing log fire to my back and nothing but the spotlights over the counter lighting my notebook, I would sit alone for hours, scribbling thoughts, plots and twists. A long day and evening serving beverages to the customers usually inspired plenty of ideas which would be promptly jotted down on a beer mat to be transcribed, explored and expanded upon after closing time.

Alas, such productive nights couldn't last, and entering public office in June 2009 and getting married that September meant that late nights in the bar came to an end. *Secrets of a Moonlit River* would possibly have remained a secret (and unfinished) had it not been for a cycling trip to beautiful Cleggan and Inisbofin in County Galway, in August 2011. There, I found freedom of mind and inspiration to continue what I'd started four years earlier, and even plan some new works.

A year later, a temporary back injury and the wet, wet August of 2012 conspired to allow the finishing touches to be added. Finally, what had originally started out as a short story became the novel you're now holding in your hands.

I hope you enjoy the story, wherever and whenever you may be reading it.

Brendan Griffin
November 2013

CHAPTER ONE

The Moloneys stood together in a row at the gate of their terraced house to see Cathal off. Mrs Moloney wept, while her husband and young son waved emotionally, as the ageing red Toyota Carina pulled away noisily, emitting a plume of thick smoke into the chill November air. Although inwardly he was frightened like never before in his thirteen-year-old life, Cathal waved back enthusiastically, his head and upper body stretching out the passenger window.

As his grandfather's car rounded the corner of Marian Terrace and O'Shea Road, Cathal lost sight of the Moloneys and the house next door, the house where he had grown up, where he had many a cherished memory but which now, through its emptiness, represented the ultimate tragedy, loss and sorrow. 2013 had turned out to be the unluckiest year imaginable for Cathal and now he gulped with uneasy anticipation, not knowing what lay ahead.

Cathal barely knew his grandfather. A low-sized man in his mid-seventies, Granda carried a sizeable pot belly but seemed thin everywhere else on his body. His hairline had receded considerably, from Cathal's earlier memories of him, and now only a rim of snow-white hair covered a crescent-shaped patch from one ear to the other around the back of his head, leaving his shiny crown as bald as an egg.

Granda was now Cathal's only close living relative. Since the death of his parents and only brother, forty-three days earlier, Cathal had taken up temporary residence with his next-door neighbours while his grandfather made alterations to his own home to accommodate his grandson on a permanent basis.

Granda hadn't featured much in Cathal's life up until the tragedy. In fact, the boy could only recall a few encounters ever with him. These were usually at Christmas time, when he would call for a half an hour, or maybe less, sometimes leaving a present for him and his brother, sometimes not. On one particular occasion, when Cathal was very young, Granda and Cathal's father, who was Granda's son, argued bitterly. Granda didn't visit again for a couple of years.

Not many words were spoken between the pair as they left the town and headed for the countryside. Cathal initially thought that it was just shyness on his grandfather's part, but soon realised that it was probably the old man's nervousness whilst driving in an urban area that caused the lack of conversation, with every ounce of Granda's concentration being focussed on manoeuvring the roundabouts, traffic lights and slip lanes that came his way.

At one stage, a lengthy queue of traffic built up behind Granda's car, as he slowly made his way along. The hooting and flashing of some impatient motorists forced him to pull over to the side of the road after a few minutes to allow the tailback to clear. Cathal was mortified in the passenger seat, hiding his face with his hand for fear of being recognised. However, once they moved out to the single-lane roads of the open countryside, Granda was visibly more relaxed and began to talk to his grandson.

"I'm glad I'm out of that town. I never liked town driving," he exclaimed in his strong Kerry accent.

"Tell me this, Cathal, have you ever been to Ballycastle before?"

"Just passing through on the way to the beach, Granda, but I never saw your house."

"Ah, you wouldn't if you were just passing through going to the beach. I'm well off the beaten track, up at the foot of the mountain where nobody bothers me."

"How well off the beaten track are you exactly, Granda?" Cathal asked with some concern in his voice.

"Oh, don't worry. It's nice and secluded but, sure, I've great neighbours only a few hundred yards away."

Cathal knew from school that a yard was close enough to a metre and, given that the house where he grew up was attached to his neighbours' house, the thought of living a few hundred yards away from his nearest neighbour was totally alien, if not a little frightening.

"Don't worry, Cathal, you'll be very happy living with me," Granda said reassuringly, before sympathetically adding, "well, as happy as you can be."

As they continued on towards their destination, parts of the countryside and certain landmarks were familiar to Cathal from previous excursions in happier times with his parents. He recognised a monument to a War of Independence soldier that his father had told him about and noticed a huge house with a long, fancy driveway that his mother had once marvelled at.

Passing through the village of Ballycastle, Cathal recognised the beautiful stone church with its picturesque churchyard, and McCarthy's Bar with its distinctive thatched roof, as well as the GAA grounds with the black and amber colours of Ballycastle flying proudly on a flag hoisted high above the entrance gates. He also noticed - to his disappointment - that the reception bars on his mobile phone disappeared on arriving in Ballycastle and that 'No Service' was now permanently displayed in the top left corner of his screen.

"It won't be long now," Granda announced, as the Carina climbed over a steep, humpback bridge and around a narrow bend in the road.

On the left, just after the bend, was the school, a stone building with a solitary door in the centre and four high-positioned windows on either side of the door that made it impossible to see what was happening inside or, for that matter, made it impossible for those inside to see what was happening outside.

"That's where you'll go to school, Cathal," Granda proudly explained. "Your father went there before you and I went there before him. And before that, my father went there."

"Gee, how old is it?" Cathal gasped.

Not noticing the cynical tone of Cathal's question, Granda went on to deliver a comprehensive history of the two-classroom building, of how it was built just after the famine in 1850, of how the Black and Tans tried to burn it down in the early 1920s but the locals, including Cathal's great-great-grandfather, stopped them with force. He told of how it was closed down for a week in 1981 when vandals smashed the windows and of how the votes of every local at every election since the foundation of the State had been cast within its walls.

Granda's lecture on St Joseph's National School was cut short when he approached a narrow, untarred bohereen that led from the main road towards the mountain. The roadway was barely wide enough for Granda's car to turn into and as they proceeded uphill over the rocky surface, which had grass growing in the centre, the trees and briars that grew along the verges reached out and scratched the sides of the already aged-looking vehicle.

"We're on the home stretch now," Granda excitedly informed his companion.

After what seemed like an eternity to Cathal, the briars and branches finally gave way to a clearing and there, about one hundred metres ahead, he could see a long, low, whitewashed cottage, with small, red wooden windows, a red front door and smoke rising from the solitary chimney. It wasn't quite what Cathal had expected, but it looked homely and, for the first time, this move to the countryside to live with his grandfather did not seem so bad to him after all.

"There it is, Cathal boy, that's our home."

"It's lovely, Granda, it's like something from a postcard."

"It is and all, boy, isn't it? And the Slieve Gaum mountains rising majestically from my backyard. They're my sheds for my turkeys around at the back of the house and there's my old donkey's car," he explained, as he pointed to the left of the house, clearly glad that Cathal's first impression was positive.

The driveway led right up past the gable of the house and around to the sheds at the back where there was space to park the car. As soon as they rounded the corner, Granda slammed on the brakes. Cathal, who had been looking over his left shoulder out the passenger window at the panoramic view of the harbour, was startled and glanced at his grandfather with amazement.

"What's wrong Granda?" he asked, noticing that his grandfather's face had grown pale, his eyes fixed firmly ahead of him.

Cathal quickly looked to where his grandfather was looking and there in the backyard were two of the biggest and strongest-looking men that Cathal had ever seen, dressed all in black, with one of them holding a hurley in his hands. Their jeep was concealed behind the turf shed and the pair began to march towards the old man's car, with menacing looks on their dark, bearded faces.

~

Bang! The edge of the hurley crashed down on the bonnet of Granda's car with such force that a steady flow of steam from the radiator beneath burst into the air. The impact stunned Cathal and he felt the blood drain from his face as his whole body froze in the passenger seat.

"Out of the car, old man!" yelled the man with the hurley in a strong Dublin accent, as he moved around to the driver's door, while his accomplice moved to Cathal's side of the car.

Granda went to lock his door but, before he had time to reach the lock, the brute had swung the door open and was literally dragging the petrified senior out of his seat by the collar of his jacket.

"You get out when I tell you to get out, old man!" shouted the man, his mouth only inches from Granda's ear, as he stood him up against the back car door at the driver's side.

"Take it easy, my grandson is with me," answered Granda, his voice trembling with fear as he held his hands around his ears in a protective stance.

By this stage, the other thug was dragging Cathal out of the car and around to where his grandfather was being held.

"Don't hurt him, he's just a boy," Granda yelled, as Cathal, now shaking with fear, was placed beside him.

"Just shut up and listen and nobody will get hurt," replied the man who had pulled Cathal from the car, his accent less pronounced than that of the other man, but still distinctly Dublin.

"Don't worry, Cathal, it'll be alright," Granda whispered to his grandson before the man with the hurley shouted into Granda's ear once again:

"He said shut up and when he says shut up, you shut up."

"That's enough," interrupted the other man.

"You know who's sent us here and you know why," he continued. "If our man doesn't get his money, you'll pay in other ways. You were given thirty days to pay and it's now been thirty-four. We take it from your failure to contact us that you don't have the money. You now have two more weeks, with an extra €1,500 interest. If you don't have the money then, God help you."

Bang! The hurley crashed down on the car again, this time shattering the back windscreen of the Carina, scattering glass all over Cathal's few remaining worldly possessions which were on the back seat.

With that, the two assailants turned and walked towards their jeep, laughing and sniggering as they went. As they drove past the boy and his grandfather, who were still standing in shock, the driver slowed and rolled down the window of the jeep.

"Don't forget, two weeks or else," he casually remarked, before driving down the lane with the engine roaring.

As the brutish duo drove away, Granda fell to his knees in a fit of coughing that left him gasping to catch his breath. Cathal's shock turned quickly to concern, as he tried to come to the aid of his grandfather by gently tapping him on the back to help him get his breath. He wasn't sure how this would help but it was the only thing he could think of.

"Are you okay, Granda? Are you okay?"

The old man beckoned with his left hand that he was okay, although he was still coughing violently and gasping for air, his face now the colour of red wine. He coughed and he coughed but, eventually, the coughing eased and he was able to get to his feet again, taking deep breaths as he did.

"Oh boy, oh boy," Granda exclaimed, a tone of disbelief in his voice, as he stood in his backyard, bent over, with the palms of his hands on the front of his thighs, still reeling from the attack.

"Who were those men, Granda, and what did they want?"

Granda remained silent.

"Granda, who were those men?" Cathal again asked, this time with more urgency in his voice.

"I don't know, boy. I don't know. There must have been some mistake. I've never seen those men before in my life," he replied after some hesitation.

Cathal decided that the best course of action to take would be to phone the Gardaí and report the incident to them. He pulled his mobile phone out of his pocket but quickly realised that he had no reception.

"Granda, have you a landline? We need to phone the guards," Cathal said.

"No, no, no! No guards, Cathal. No guards," Granda replied decisively.

"But, Granda, that's what the guards are there for - to stop things like this happening," Cathal protested.

"No guards, Cathal, and no is no," Granda said forcefully.

That was enough to put an end to any further suggestions from Cathal, who decided it was better not to put the old man under further pressure, although he wasn't convinced by his grandfather's plea of ignorance in relation to the motive for the attack and was bemused by his reluctance to engage the attention of the local constabulary.

He had come to Ballycastle to start a new life in a safe and protected environment yet his first experience of his new home had been a violent and frightening encounter and Cathal wondered what he was after getting himself into and if he really could depend on Granda to provide the stable home that he needed.

Before Cathal had a chance to give deeper thought to the matter, Granda had turned and made his way to where he had left his car. Sitting into the driver's seat, he tried a few times to start the engine, but the damage that had been carried out in the attack had obviously caused some serious problem and the car would not budge.

"We'll have to push it the few yards into the shed," Granda

stated. "You steer and I'll push, Cathal," he added, beckoning the boy to take his place at the wheel of the car. "Now, when I say so, release the handbrake," Granda instructed.

Cathal had never sat behind the wheel of a real car before, but he knew how to operate a handbrake. On the count of three, Granda shouted the word "now" and Cathal released the handbrake. He felt the car moving slowly as his grandfather pushed with all his might from the rear of the vehicle.

"Steer, Cathal, steer," he shouted, as the old banger neared the wall of the shed and, with all his strength, Cathal managed to turn the stiff, old steering wheel just in time to guide the car through the open shed door.

"Brake, Cathal, brake!" shouted Granda, as the Carina headed for the back wall of the shed but, with a mighty heave, Cathal somehow managed to bring the car to a halt, inches from the blockwork.

"Good man. Grab your stuff there, lad, and we'll get you settled into your new home," he instructed the youngster as he reached into the back seat of the car and pulled out Cathal's bags.

The boy took his bags from his grandfather's hands after he had shaken off the tiny cubes of broken glass that were spread all over them after the thugs' final act of vandalism. He was shocked at what had just happened and this shock was now compounded by his grandfather's mysterious reaction.

"Follow me, so," Granda said, as he turned and pulled the keys from the ignition of the car and walked towards the back door of the cottage. Granda's hand was visibly shaking as he tried to put the key of the door in the lock. In fact, the shaking was so uncontrollable that he had to use his left hand to guide his right hand to successfully place the key in the lock.

Eventually, the key was turned and the little wooden door creaked open to reveal a small and bleak, pale pink-coloured room with nothing in it but a stand-alone cooker, refrigerator and a stainless steel sink with two wooden presses underneath. A pair of muddy, black wellington boots was carefully placed on the white linoleum floor just inside the door and a tank of cooking gas sat beside the cooker.

They both entered, Granda leading the way, with Cathal very nervously looking over his shoulder as he went through the door, hoping that no further nasty surprises awaited him inside the house.

"This is my little kitchen, lad. I do all my cooking in here. And in here is the living room," Granda explained as he led Cathal through the first room into a larger, and more comfortable, second room.

The living room was bright and spacious. The centrepiece of the room was a big open fireplace, complete with a huge wooden mantelpiece, a large black iron crane and a fine big grate, where a small turf fire was now dwindling, its smoke giving the room a strong but sweet aroma.

"I'd better throw some more turf on the fire before it goes out," observed Granda, noticing Cathal surveying the situation.

Granda placed two sods of turf on the fire before guiding his grandson around the most important room in the house.

"Here is our table," he proudly declared, hitting the solid oak surface with the base of his clasped fist.

"And over here is the telly with channels one, two, three and four."

"No Sky Sports?" Cathal quizzed.

"Sky what?"

"Sky Sports, you know - for all the soccer and other sports?"

"Sure, isn't there plenty of that on these channels. I don't be watchin' it much anyway, it kinda hurts my eyes, you know," he said dismissively, before he continued with his tour, all the time possessing an element of uneasiness which was a direct consequence of the earlier confrontation.

"And over here at the window you have a fine view of the River Clane and Ballycastle Harbour, with the town of Killcrown across the water in the distance and the McCarthy Reeks Mountains in the background. Closer to us is Murphy's Estate and Woods and Killcrown Pier.

"In the middle of the woods there's a grand big estate house and the woods are said to be haunted. On this side of the water you have Ballycastle Pier and down there is Coill na Marbh Woods. Those woods are supposed to be haunted, too, but I'll tell you about that another time."

Cathal was fascinated by this. Always one with a sense of adventure, he felt himself bubbling with excitement as soon as he heard the reference to hauntings.

"You mean with real ghosts, Granda?"

"Well, what other type of ghosts are there?"

"Wow. Have you ever seen them?"

"Not personally, no. But I do know a few people who have seen some strange things in the woods."

"Wow, like what?"

"Well, strange things, unusual things."

"Such as what, Granda?" Cathal asked with excitement.

"Ah, you know, strange things - lights and strange stuff."

"Tell me more!"

"Ah no, I'd be afraid 'twud frighten you."

"No it wouldn't, Granda, I love ghost stories."

"Except these aren't stories, these are real events, so I'll say no more for now."

Cathal was dying to hear more but, not being a cheeky boy and still being relatively newly acquainted with his grandfather, he decided to let the subject pass, for a while.

"Most of the food is kept in here, down low, and the cups and plates up high," Granda announced, as he continued with his tour, pointing to an old white wooden dresser in the corner of the room, with two small, stiff drawers for cutlery and tea towels.

Cathal scanned the room, trying to take in as much as he could. In one corner, a large grandfather clock stood majestically on the floor, taller than him or his grandfather, and producing a grand and solid tick-tock. Cathal found it amusing as he privately figured that his grandfather's grandfather clock must have been Cathal's own great-great-grandfather clock.

His attention was caught by some framed photographs hanging on the wall but before he had a chance to ask any questions or look at who was in the photos, Granda was ushering him through the next door into a narrow and dark entrance hallway, with brown linoleum flooring and bright pink walls.

"My bedroom is through that door there, lad," he declared, as he pointed straight across the hallway to the door just beside the bottom of the stairs.

"The bathroom door is around at the back of the stairs. Your room is up the stairs and to the left. Up you go," he said enthusiastically, as he allowed Cathal to lead the way up the narrow, creaking steps to his new sleeping quarters. At the top of the stairs, there were two doors, one to the left and one to the right.

"You're into the left, Cathal boy," Granda reminded him, as the boy reached the landing.

Cathal wasn't quite sure what to expect as he placed his hand on the small wooden doorknob. Anxiously, he turned the knob and opened the door to reveal his new bedroom. He stood for a moment at the door, surveying the scene. Immediately, Cathal was enthused by the character and layout of what was a slightly dark, yet spacious, loft room.

It was warm and cosy and had loads more space than Cathal's last bedroom in his parents' house. In the gable wall at the far end of the room, a small sliding sash window allowed a great view of the surrounding landscape and, beside the window, there was a wooden writing desk and seat, complete with a lamp and storage drawers.

A large wardrobe stood just beside the door and the black metal-frame bed was positioned midway in the room, with the head of the bed tucked in under the northern slope of the roof. In fact, the roof came right down to the floor of the room on two sides and Cathal had to duck his head as he placed his bags on the floor beside his bed.

"I hope you like it, Cathal, I had it done up 'specially for you."

"Like it? I love it. It's really cool, Granda. I love it."

"Cool? Sure it's roasting up here. You're right above the fireplace," Granda replied in disbelief, showing a distinct lack of understanding of Cathal's vocabulary.

Cathal considered explaining the misunderstanding but thought it easier to just smile and express satisfaction with the bedroom.

"It's perfect, Granda, just perfect. Thank you."

Granda smiled. He had been anxious for weeks about the impression that his humble cottage would make on his new lodger, but now a great sense of relief and achievement allowed him to relax and enjoy the occasion.

Suddenly, the loud sound of smashing glass came from downstairs. Cathal looked at Granda and the old man stared back at his grandson. The tour of the house had temporarily distracted both of them from the drama that had occurred just a short time earlier in the backyard but, now, fear and nervousness gripped the pair again. They both wondered if the thugs had come back and whether they were inside the house this time.

~

"What was that?" Cathal whispered to his grandfather, who was equally fearful of the cause of the sudden mysterious clatter.

"I don't know, boy."

"Maybe those men have come back, Granda?"

"I don't know, boy. You stay here. I'd better go to find out."

"No, I'll go, Granda. It'd be safer".

"What do you mean - it'd be safer?"

"Well, I'm just a kid, they'd hardly harm me."

"Hardly harm you? My boy, you don't know what these people are capable of."

"There it is again," Cathal thought.

Granda seemed to know more about the suspected intruders than he originally had declared to know but, this aside, his grandson instantly took the decisive action of going to see who or what had caused the noise downstairs. Before Granda had a chance to change his grandson's mind, Cathal was tiptoeing down the squeaky and rickety stairs, leaving the old man behind to nervously ponder the logic of the boy's actions.

As he made his way closer to the living room, he felt a tingling up his spine and every breath he took seemed to come from the very depths of his lungs. As he approached the door, he listened intently to what might be going on at the other side. He thought that he could hear footsteps and the clinking of broken glass.

He had just placed his ear to the old wooden door when, all of a sudden, it opened and Cathal roared with fright. Granda, who by now was halfway down the stairs, raced to the scene the instant he heard his grandson's yelp, which had been met with an equally loud female shrieking.

There, at the entrance to the living room, Granda was relieved to see Cathal standing opposite Peggy Moore, a neighbour, who had taken the liberty of letting herself in. Both stood facing each other in silence before Granda's arrival brought some normality back to the situation.

"It's okay, Cathal, it's okay, Peggy is a friend of mine," he said reassuringly.

"It's okay Cathal? What about poor me and the life and it half scared out of me by this little guerrilla?"

"Gorilla?" responded Cathal, taking exception to the comment.

"Yes, guerrilla, as in one who ambushes people," she clarified.

"I didn't ambush you. I just heard a noise and was going to see what it was."

"Well, you frightened the wits out of me whatever you were doing," she proclaimed, with her arms folded defensively in front of her very large frame.

A woman in her mid-sixties, Peggy always seemed to be more interested in everybody else's business than her own. Her full-length blue coat and her floral head scarf left only her face to be seen, a particularly apt dress code for a woman who shrouded her life and affairs from the attention of others while observing all that was going on around her.

"Peggy, allow me to introduce you to my grandson, Cathal. Cathal, this is my friend and neighbour, Peggy Moore," said Granda, full of officialdom.

"Pleased to meet you, ma'am," said Cathal, reaching out his right hand to the stout woman.

"It certainly is a meeting I won't forget for a long time," remarked Peggy, stretching out her hand to meet that of the boy, adding that she was sorry for his recent troubles.

"I'm sorry, Peggy, we were upstairs getting Cathal settled into his new room and we didn't hear you knocking."

"Well, I couldn't knock because my hands were full at the

time," she said, "so I let myself in. I was trying to turn the doorknob coming into the living room when I dropped the bowl of trifle that I had made for the new arrival."

"So that's what we heard," blurted Cathal.

"Well, it's no use to man or mouse now because it's all over the living room floor, along with my Pyrex bowl. A wedding present for Jack Moore and myself it was, God be good to him."

"Sure it must have been well gone sour if 'twas a wedding present you got it for, Peg!" joked Granda.

"I was talking about the bowl, Mick Kavanagh. The trifle I made fresh this very morning," responded Peggy, not appreciating the wit in Granda's comment.

"Well, I suppose, it'd be worse if it was a new one," Granda added humorously in reference to the antique bowl, to which Peggy offered no response, only a piercing stare followed by a speedy shift of subject.

"So, young man, this is your new home now. I hope you behave yourself around the parish and don't be causing a nuisance for your grandfather or anybody else," she lectured, as if she had authority to do so.

She continued: "I hope that you appreciate the trouble your grandfather has had to get the house ready for you."

Then, turning to Granda, she said: "Did you say that Cathal's room upstairs is ready, Mick?"

Granda barely had time to confirm the news when Peggy had powered past him and Cathal and pounded straight up the stairs to see the work for herself, the steps thundering and creaking under the pressure of her body as she made her determined ascent.

"A grand job alright, Mick, a grand job," she shouted from the room door down the stairs to the pair who were still standing in the small hallway, with Cathal amazed by the sheer nosiness and inquisitiveness of this woman.

"I suppose it must have cost you a small fortune, Mick?" she quizzed at the top of her voice, still standing at the door of the room, making a detailed mental note of all that lay before her.

"Ah, it wasn't too bad, Peg," Granda replied, not wanting to divulge any further information and feeling rather awkward about the question, especially for fear that it would impress upon Cathal that he was in some way a financial burden.

"How much?" she asked brazenly.

Cathal threw his eyes up to heaven in disbelief at her boldness.

"I don't remember, Peggy, but if I do, you'll be the first to know," Granda responded with sarcasm, hoping that it would be enough to repel the barrage of rapid-fire questions.

Although his comment was enough to stop Peggy enquiring further into the subject of the room refurbishment, her attention now shifted to the other upstairs room, as she moved across the landing and grabbed the doorknob opposite Cathal's room door. Her attempts to open the door were in vain, however, as the door was locked shut.

"What's in this room, Mick?" she yelled, still rattling the doorknob.

Granda looked at Cathal anxiously and then glanced up at Peggy, who was now staring down at him.

"Nothing in there, Peggy, just an empty bit of storage space. Haven't been in there in years."

Peggy assessed his every facial expression, as if trying to establish whether he was telling the truth or not, and then began making her way back down the stairs, the entire house vibrating with every step of her descent.

"Well, I'll be off now," she declared as she brushed past Cathal and his grandfather once again and re-entered the living room. They followed her and were met by the sight of the shattered trifle bowl, with its contents scattered all over the floor.

"Get the boy to clean it up, Mick," she ordered, as she stepped over the debris and made her way out the back door of the cottage to where she had parked her shiny red Nissan Micra, complete with the first-day plastic film still covering the seats, even though the car was more than ten years old.

"By the way," she shouted back to Granda, who had followed her as far as the doorway of the cottage, "who were those men that passed by here earlier in the big wagon, Mick?"

"Ah, they were, ah, just selling some stuff, Peggy," he responded with much hesitation and uncertainty.

"What type of stuff?" she inquired immediately.

"Ah, not sure. Not sure, Peggy, wasn't interested - full stop."

Peggy fixed her lie-assessment stare on him for a few seconds before sitting into her car and heading off about the rest of her day's business, leaving the yard almost as fast as the two thugs.

Granda returned to the living room where Cathal had started cleaning up the mess left after Peggy's accident.

"You didn't have to do that because she said so, you know," Granda said to the boy, who had the task nearly completed by that stage.

"It's no problem really, Granda," Cathal replied as he scooped up the last of the mess.

"Well, that was the great Peggy Moore - local investigator, interrogator, reporter, newscaster, and outright gossip," Granda announced.

"She is rather domineering alright."

"Don't worry, they're not all like that around here, although it's very hard to keep anything private in Ballycastle. Now go and get your bags unpacked and I'll start dinner. We have a lot to talk about tonight."

Cathal made his way upstairs and into his room. His grandfather was right. They did have a lot to talk about, especially what had happened earlier in the backyard and what it was those men really wanted. Cathal was determined to find out.

∽

LATER IN THE EVENING, after Cathal had unpacked his bags and settled into his new room, the pair sat down for a meal of bacon, cabbage and potatoes which Granda prepared in his basic, yet productive, kitchen.

The blazing log and turf fire in the open fireplace chased away the darkness and coldness of the world outside and Cathal felt very cosy in his new surroundings. He began to feel that he was much more comfortable with his grandfather, whom he hardly knew, than he had been with the Moloneys, with whom he had stayed for the six weeks since his parents and brother died, although he had known them all of his life, and despite the fact that they had been extremely kind and generous to him. For the first time since the tragedy, Cathal had a feeling that things would be alright and that he somehow belonged in the hillside cottage.

He had so much that he wanted to ask his grandfather, so, during dinner, he decided that he was going to try and find out the information that he was looking for.

"Granda."

"Yes, Cathal."

"I have a few questions that I want to ask you."

"Ask me anything, lad."

"Okay, well, first of all, how come you weren't around much in the past, like other grandfathers?" Cathal asked in a frank, yet non-accusing, manner.

"Well," said Granda, as he sat upright in his chair opposite his grandson, "that's a good question. I suppose the truth being told, it was a problem that existed between your father and myself. He was my only child and I loved him as any father would love his son, and he thought the same about me also, I think. It's just that, well, we didn't really see eye to eye all the time, in fact, any of the time, really. It's strange the way families are sometimes. Anyway, even though we never really acknowledged it, we both seemed to think that the less we saw of each other the better it would be. I know it probably is hard for you to try to understand that, but it worked best for us."

"It is hard to understand. Didn't you miss him and us?"

"Of course, of course I did," he replied, with deep sincerity in his voice, as he placed a huge lump of butter on his potatoes. "It's just that it was easier to do it the way we did. Of course, I never thought that I would outlive my own son, daughter-in-law and grandson, but I wasn't to know what would happen. If I had the chance again, I would do everything differently, but that's life, I suppose. It's hard, thinking about what happened. Although I didn't have much contact with your parents and your brother and you in recent years, I miss them something fierce now. We still had a family bond, and that never breaks, Cathal. Always remember that."

"Do you think they'd have wanted me to come live with you, Granda?"

The old man thought for a moment, chewing his bacon as he pondered.

"That's a very good question to be asking, Cathal, but I think that they'd be happy, yes. It's strange, but when your grandmother - my wife - died, your father was only thirteen years old also. I think that event brought us much closer together as a father and son, yet, at the same time, kept us apart in a way that I don't really understand. In fact, it's nice for me to be having this conversation with you because I never found myself able to talk this openly with your father, nor he with me. It's a pity, but men can be like that sometimes, I think. Do you understand what I'm saying?"

"I think so, Granda. It's just that, I really feel at home here and I'm only here a few hours."

"And so you should, Cathal. After all, you'll be sleeping tonight in the very bedroom where your father spent the first twenty years of his life. He loved that room. It was his space and now it's fitting that you should have it."

Both were silent for a few moments before Cathal began again.

"There's one other thing I want to ask about, Granda."

"What's that, Cathal?"

"Those men today, Granda, they really frightened me," Cathal said timidly. "Why didn't you call the guards on them?"

Granda was silent. He looked at Cathal, who knew from his grandfather's reaction that he had trouble answering the question. After a few moments of silence, Cathal fixed his eyes on his dinner plate in an attempt to escape the awkwardness of the situation but Granda finally responded to the question.

"It's complicated, Cathal, and I won't lie to you anymore, I did know those men today and I owe them a small sum of money that I got from them on loan. All I will say, though, is that I have the matter under control and that it is nothing at all for you to be concerned about. I can assure you that what happened today will not happen again."

Cathal looked at his grandfather and then, realising that he himself was now adopting a Peggy Moore-style lie-assessment stare, fixed his eyes back onto his dinner plate, where very little of the meal remained. Cathal was far from satisfied by the answer that he had received, but he decided to let the matter drop for now, given the sense of awkwardness that it evoked.

When dinner was finished and Cathal had helped with his share of the washing up and cleaning, the two sat beside the fire, drinking cups of tea and munching on some of Granda's favourite butter cookies, which Cathal took an instant liking to. They chatted for hours about all sorts of subjects and stories until the grandfather clock struck 10pm and it was time for Cathal to go to bed.

"Time you were turning in, young man, you have a big day ahead of you tomorrow with your first day at St Joseph's National School," Granda said, as he rose to his feet and placed the spark guard in front of the fire.

Cathal, who was exhausted after his day, had hardly even thought about starting in his new school. He hadn't even tried on the new school uniform that Granda had left hanging in the wardrobe in his bedroom, or looked at the books in his new schoolbag. Now, however, the prospect of transferring to a new school, mid-term, where he would know nobody, was looming and began to seem quite daunting.

Cathal bid goodnight to his grandfather and dragged his weary body up the stairs to his bedroom. Despite his strange surroundings and his apprehension about the day that lay ahead, he felt tiredness like never before. Once ready, he turned off the light and lay into his new bed with its crisp white sheets. The sound of the winter rain falling softly on the roof gave him a feeling of great warmth and cosiness and within minutes of his head touching his pillow, he was asleep.

~

LATER THAT NIGHT, something woke Cathal. When he opened his heavy and sleepy eyes, he could make out in the darkness that his digital clock radio read 2.06am. He sat up in the bed and wiped his eyes, initially confused regarding his surroundings until he remembered that he was at his grandfather's. He thought that he could hear a strange crackling noise, rather like the sound of breaking twigs. He listened again and, this time, he was sure that he could hear a voice. It was a woman's voice and it was coming from somewhere in the house. It seemed to be calling his name in a faint, whispery echo: "Cathal, Cathal, Cathal."

He listened again in the darkness, his heart pounding and, sure enough, there was the mysterious voice again, only this time, it seemed further away and less clear, although still calling his name: "Cathal, Cathal, Cathal." He listened but the voice faded away into the night until, finally, he could no longer hear it. However, the strange crackling sound grew louder and it seemed like a hurricane had suddenly gathered outside.

Cathal felt the hairs standing on the back of his neck the moment he noticed the distinctive smell of smoke as it seeped into the bedroom from under his door. He jumped out of bed to find that the room was already filled with thick, black smoke which filled his lungs as he tried to breathe. He somehow managed to make his way through the smoke and darkness to the door, but his worst fears were realised when he opened it and saw that the entire house was engulfed in roaring flames.

He was in the middle of a raging inferno and all he could do was scream for help at the top of his voice.

~

GRANDA WAS FAST ASLEEP DOWNSTAIRS when he heard his grandson's hysterical calls for help coming from the loft bedroom. He leapt out of bed and raced out of his room and up the stairs towards Cathal's bedroom. The boy was still frantically shouting for help as Granda flung the door open and turned on the light.

There, before him, he found his grandson sitting upright in his bed, clutching the bed sheets to his chest, his hair damp with perspiration, his face pale and petrified. He was still calling for help as Granda rushed to his side to comfort him and bring him to his senses.

"It's alright, Cathal, it's alright," Granda declared, as he threw his arms around the boy in an effort to calm his hysteria.

"The fire! The fire!" Cathal screamed, his head now shifting from left to right, as if searching his surroundings for the blaze, still clutching the bed sheets to his chest with his clenched fists.

"There's no fire, Cathal," Granda interrupted, "you're with me and you're safe. There's no fire. Everything is alright."

After a few moments of continued distress and panic, Cathal fell silent and, realising his whereabouts and that he had just had a terrible nightmare, he burst into tears and cried bitterly on his grandfather's shoulder.

"It's alright, Cathal, it's alright. Let it out, you'll be alright," Granda said consolingly, as a combination of fear, mourning, confusion and loneliness overwhelmed the boy.

Cathal cried himself to sleep that night while his grandfather sat on the edge of his bed watching over him. The bereavement counsellor had warned Granda that he could expect such episodes occasionally but that Cathal would get all the support he needed to help him through his terrible and difficult loss. After all, such emotional trauma was to be expected from a boy who had lost his brother, mother and father in a horrific house fire just over a month earlier.

∼

CATHAL WOKE IN THE MORNING to a much more hospitable situation than his nightmarish awakening of a few hours earlier. The aroma of frying rashers and sausages filtered into his room and filled his nostrils. Despite having eaten a huge meal the evening before, the smell of the Irish breakfast made his mouth water and he was up, dressed and ready in minutes and made his way to the breakfast table, rigged out in his new school uniform. On the table before him lay the most unbelievable breakfast he had ever seen.

"Good morning, young man, and aren't you looking the clever bucko today," remarked Granda, as he sat proudly at the top of the table, his breakfast plate loaded to the brim in front of him.

"Hi Granda," Cathal replied in amazement, his eyes fixed on the great meal that sat before him.

"That's the best breakfast you'll get from here to Timbuktu, boy, so tuck in and you won't be hungry for the day."

"I won't be hungry for a week if I eat that," replied Cathal as he picked up his cutlery, trying to decide where to start.

Would he start with the sausages, rashers, black pudding, white pudding, fried eggs, fried tomato, beans, fried mushrooms, fried potato, or maybe the toast? This was a breakfast to savour. Cathal duly attacked the monstrous breakfast and no-one spoke for at least five minutes, as they both devoured their delicious food.

While pouring the tea, Granda asked Cathal how he was feeling after the traumatic nightmare he'd had during the night.

"Well, are you okay?"

"I'm really sorry about last night, Granda," Cathal replied sadly.

"Don't be daft, boy, you have nothing to be sorry about. We all have bad dreams sometimes."

"It was just so awful, Granda. The house was on fire all around me and I could hear my mother calling my name and, before I knew it, I was calling for help."

"It must have been awful," Granda agreed, as he loaded his tea with three heaped spoons of sugar, before giving a loud and lengthy stir.

"Don't ever be afraid to talk to me about anything like that, Cathal, that's important, you know."

"I know, Granda, I won't."

"And when you're sad or upset, there's nothing wrong with having a good cry for yourself or telling me all about it."

"Okay, Granda," Cathal agreed gratefully.

"Now," said Granda, as he lifted the mood, "get the rest of Mick Kavanagh's famous full Irish breakfast into you and we'll make our way to school. You're goin' to have a great day today, lad."

When all was consumed, Cathal could hardly move as he left the breakfast table to put on his coat and fetch his schoolbag.

"Come on so, Cathal, it's time we were on our way," announced Granda, as he made his way to the back door and out into the backyard.

With the car out of action since the vandalism of the previous day, Cathal wondered how they would be travelling to school, which was about two kilometres away from the cottage. His curiosity was soon answered when Granda made his way to the far side of the backyard and swung open the two wooden barn doors. There, parked up in all its glory was Granda's tractor, a small red Massey Ferguson, facing outward, ready to embark on its next call of duty.

The tractor had no official registration plate but written neatly on to the front grill in white paint was '35 KY 16'.

"This tractor is older than Granda," Cathal thought to himself.

Granda climbed up on the old machine and helped Cathal up beside him, putting the boy sitting on the metal rear mudguard with his hands clasping the iron roll bar. The key was already in the ignition and Granda prepared to turn it, pressing the clutch and putting the tractor into neutral gear.

"Here we go, Cathal, hold on tight," Granda exclaimed, as he turned the key in the ignition.

Nothing happened.

Granda looked at his grandson with a slightly embarrassed chuckle before attempting to start the ignition again.

Nothing happened again.

"Must be cold," Granda said anxiously, as he prepared to turn the key for a third time but, again, nothing happened.

"Bugger that anyway," Granda cursed, realising that the tractor wasn't going anywhere.

The pair sat silently on the tractor for a few moments before Granda announced what he called 'Plan C'. Cathal had no idea what that would be. However, after disembarking from the tractor and following his grandfather through the farmyard to yet more outhouses, it soon dawned on Cathal what Granda meant by Plan C.

CHAPTER TWO

The school yard was alive with the energetic morning play of the students of St Joseph's National School. Many of the smaller children darted to and fro in a game that involved a tennis ball and a cardboard box, while some of the older children were bunched in groups of threes and fours, discussing their respective topics of importance.

On the small green area beside the yard, a group of about ten boys were playing a fiercely competitive game of soccer, with another group of ten contesting a basketball match on the small court at the far end of the yard. The main entrance of the school was busy with cars arriving to drop off children for the day ahead and more children were arriving on bicycles, their knuckles red from the sharp morning air.

As they drew close to the school, Cathal began to hear the excited voices of the playing children. The sound grew louder and louder until, eventually, he and his grandfather rounded a bend in the road, after which the school came into view. Cathal gulped with anticipation, his nervousness exasperated by his emergency mode of transport, which he feared would attract some unwanted attention.

He surveyed the school as they approached the entrance and was slightly intimidated by the sight of so many children at play with their peers. However, his worst fear was realised when he saw a small boy run towards the school gate, as if in slow motion, his arm outstretched with his finger pointing straight at Cathal and his grandfather.

"Look, it's a donkey!" cried the little boy, his mouth wide open with amazement at what he was seeing.

Within an instant, every child in the school yard ceased what they had been doing and dashed towards the school wall from where they laughed uncontrollably at Cathal and his grandfather arriving to school on the back of a two-wheeled cart pulled by a donkey that seemed to be older than the old man holding the reins.

Cathal felt his face burning up with embarrassment and mortification. The collective laughter hit him like stones, his vulnerability exploited by sheer childish heartlessness. Plan C had turned into a disaster. 'Paddy' the donkey had gotten him to school, but Cathal was now regretting not having volunteered to walk the journey. In fact, he would have crawled, had he known the reception that he would get at the school gate.

"Don't worry, boy, you'll be grand out when they get to know you," whispered Granda, sensing the youngster's total discomfort, and now feeling a tremendous sense of guilt for having created the spectacle in the first place.

The laughter prevailed for what seemed like an eternity until the sound of a bell and the protesting voice of a woman caused the children to quickly disperse from their vantage points along the school wall.

"That's enough, that's enough - into class, into class!" cried the woman in a stern voice.

With the children scampering through the front door of the building, silence fell over the yard and Cathal felt some sense of relief. There, at the school gate was an attractive young woman, of about twenty-five, holding a large brass bell with a wooden handle.

Her black pinstriped trouser suit looked smart on her tall, thin figure. Her jet-black hair was neatly tied in a bun on top of her head, making her dark-framed spectacles a very prominent feature on her face. Her entire demeanour oozed authority, yet there was an innate kindness about her that Cathal could sense.

"You must be Cathal Kavanagh," she gently said, with sympathy in her voice and in her eyes, as the boy nodded back shyly in confirmation.

"I'm Miss O'Shea and you're welcome to St Joseph's."

"Thank you, Miss O'Shea, thank you. I'm very sorry about the donkey. The car and the tractor are out of order," Granda explained apologetically.

"Don't worry about it, Mick. Sure you're here now anyway. Are you ready, Cathal?"

Cathal and his grandfather looked at each other for a brief moment before the old man stretched out his right hand, his left hand still holding the reins.

"Good luck, boy. You'll be fine."

Cathal anxiously shook his grandfather's powerful, coarse hand, a look of trepidation etched on both of their faces. Then, hopping off the cart and stepping through the school gate, Cathal took a deep breath as he ventured into the unknown.

"Come with me and you'll be fine, Cathal," Miss O'Shea uttered reassuringly as she extended a warm handshake to the young boy.

The two were walking towards the front door of the school when Cathal suddenly felt an overwhelming urge to turn around and run back to the gate to where his grandfather had remained, watching. On seeing him rush towards the gate, Granda and Miss O'Shea feared the worst, thinking that Cathal had lost the courage to begin his new school life. However, both were relieved when they learned his motive.

"Granda, there's no need to collect me at 3pm, I'll walk home this evening. I know the way and I'll be fine," exclaimed Cathal.

Granda was a bit surprised but quickly figured that the reason for Cathal's desire to walk home stemmed from a fear of any further humiliation that could arise by continued association with the donkey. Understanding his predicament, the old man agreed to the proposal without debate.

"Okay, I'll see you at home. Just be careful and come straight home," were his instructions.

Cathal agreed and, with that, returned to the school door, where Miss O'Shea was waiting patiently.

"Alright, Cathal. Follow me and I'll show you to your classroom," she said, leading the new student through the front door and into the school.

The corridor was long, dark and grey, with worn navy-blue tiles underfoot. The only light entering the area was through narrow rectangular windows positioned high up near the ceiling. The dullness of the corridor was broken only by a small selection of colourful educational posters, covering everything from the food pyramid to the Safe Cross Code but, overall, there was an institutional feel to the place.

Miss O'Shea led Cathal past one classroom before finally arriving at the room at the end of the corridor. On the door was a sign reading '3rd, 4th, 5th and 6th class' and Cathal knew he had reached his destination. She proceeded to open the door but, rather than walking in and taking command of the class, Miss O'Shea poked her head around the solid wooden door as if to get somebody's attention, and then she closed it again.

With that, she left Cathal at the door, wishing him the very best of luck, saying, "The Master will see you shortly". She walked away from him, down the corridor and disappeared through the other classroom door. Cathal had felt secure and at ease in her presence, even though his encounter with her was so brief and he was sorry when he realised that she would not be his teacher.

After about a minute of standing alone in anticipation in the corridor, Cathal's classroom door opened and the Master appeared before him. Wearing a dull, grey tweed suit, an off-white shirt with a worn collar and a dull, grey tie, the Master was a tall, thin man. He had a wispy, grey beard that was longer on his exceptionally pointy chin than on any other part of his face. His hair was white and ruffled and had the appearance of not having been combed for a few days.

He wore a pair of thin, metal-frame, round spectacles, which were resting halfway along his extremely long nose. Between his yellow teeth, he held a cocktail stick which protruded from the side of his lips.

The Master stood opposite him, so close to the boy that Cathal felt that his personal space had been invaded. However, he felt it would be rude to take a step back to re-establish some distance between himself and the man, who was by now inspecting him from head to toe. The Master stood there in silence, judgementally looking Cathal up and down from his lofty vantage point, all the while flicking the cocktail stick with his tongue.

After a lengthy and awkward pause, the Master initiated conversation and three things immediately struck Cathal. First was that the Master had an irritatingly penetrative voice, that sounded more akin to a corncrake than a school principal. Second was that the Master had appallingly bad breath which immediately reminded Cathal of the time he had found a festering dead badger in the park.

Third, and worst of all by far, the Master had a most unsociable tendency of spitting copious quantities of saliva and other oral material as he spoke. Naturally, given the closeness of the Master to Cathal, the boy found himself sprayed from above as he squinted and turned his face in a hopeless effort to stay dry.

"So, you're Cathal Kavanagh. Son of the late, great Eamon Kavanagh and grandson of the infamous Mick Kavanagh," the Master remarked slyly.

"Yes, sir," replied Cathal promptly.

"And you're coming here to St Joseph's from the big

town, thinking you're something special?" the Master asked accusingly.

"No, sir," replied Cathal defensively, slightly rattled by the tone of the questioner.

"Well, I certainly hope not. No matter who you are or where you come from, there are no special rules for individuals at St Joseph's. There will be no special exceptions for you, no matter what your circumstances are. Is that understood, mister? You are not special," proclaimed the Master, as he jabbed his index finger into Cathal's chest on the pronouncement of the word 'special', while inadvertently discharging what seemed to be a piece of chewed cornflake that landed right between Cathal's eyes.

"Yes, sir," Cathal replied timidly, although deep inside he was bursting to challenge the dogmatic educationalist.

What was said next, however, represented a Rubicon that the Master crossed with sheer arrogance and conceit, and that drove a wedge between him and Cathal forevermore.

"I taught, or should I say, tried to teach, your father when he was a student here and he was a waster, a chancer and lazy. You'd better not turn out the same as him or God help you, boy!" he charged, with his index finger in the same mid-chest position, maintaining the same demeanour, with an increased level of venom.

Cathal was flabbergasted and simply overwhelmed by the Master's total irreverence and unprofessionalism but, try as he might to muster a meaningful comeback that would counteract the harsh words that he had just been subjected to, he was unable to utter anything other than "Yes, sir".

"Now in with you," directed the Master, as he opened

the classroom door and beckoned the boy to enter an intimidating classroom full of strangers, having just heard his father's memory dishonoured and having failed to defend him in any way.

Walking into that room, Cathal's mind was numb. He was walking into a room of twenty-five of his contemporaries, with whom he would be spending a considerable amount of time from that moment on, yet his thoughts were lost in the detail of the outrageously vile verbal assault that had just taken place in the gloomy main corridor of his new school. Signs were that Cathal's St Joseph's experience was going to be eventful.

~

CATHAL WASN'T QUITE IN TUNE with his personal environment as he took his seat in the classroom. All he knew was that he was there and that he needed to snap out of the Master-induced daze in which he found himself. He kept thinking to himself that this man was not fit to teach children and he couldn't believe that someone like him could be in such a position of authority in this day and age.

He looked around his surroundings and noticed that all eyes were on him as the Master introduced the new student to the class. What was most striking and confusing was that the Master now spoke so eloquently and positively about him, in sharp contrast with what he had encountered on the far side of the classroom door in the privacy of the corridor.

"Students, I want you all to extend a warm Ballycastle welcome to Cathal Kavanagh, who is joining our community following a recent family tragedy. I'm sure you will all do your very best to make sure that Cathal settles in well here and I hope you will all help him in any way that you can."

The classroom broke into a round of applause as a sign of welcome to their new member while the Master stared directly at Cathal with a type of domineering look that Cathal found confusing, if not downright warped. Whatever wrongdoings Cathal's father had done in his schooldays at St Joseph's, Master Seán Ó Luing had not forgotten them and seemed quite intent on inflicting revenge on the son for the sins of his father.

Either that or the Master was a complete and absolute lunatic. Cathal wasn't sure what to think, but felt it best to keep his head down and maintain a low profile in the hope that, eventually, everything would work out. After the formalities of the introduction had passed, the students were instructed to read individually in silence from their English textbooks while the Master sat at the top of the classroom reading that day's edition of the *Irish Express* newspaper.

Cathal found this method of conducting a class rather bizarre but was not going to rock the boat, so complied with the order and, as instructed, read from his textbook which had been packed carefully in his schoolbag by Granda. He found it hard to concentrate on his book, though, as his mind raced with thoughts of the earlier encounter with the Master and the subsequent manifestation of his 'alter ego'.

And then there was the matter of the student seated immediately to Cathal's right, who interrupted the silence of the classroom at ten-second intervals with a loud sniffle that would last for about two seconds every time and seemed to serve the vital purpose of preventing unsavoury and unwanted nasal outflow. It didn't take long for the Master to become aware of the sniffle, identify the perpetrator and swoop to humiliate and punish him.

"Stand up, Barty Shanahan!" the Master shouted, shattering the near-silence of the classroom, as he tipped his spectacles to the point of his nose and closed the newspaper, holding the fingers of his left hand in the previously opened pages.

Barty, who was hitherto unaware of the audibility of his overactive nasal passage, rose to his feet with a fright. Barty was in fifth class and was just after turning eleven years of age. He was short in stature for his age, but what he lacked in height, he more than made up for in width and weight. He had a generally untidy appearance, with his shirttail hanging outside his trousers and his tie knotted just above the V in his jumper, in line with the second button below his collar. The neatest aspect of his appearance was his perfectly straight ginger fringe, which was gelled onto his forehead as if it was stuck with Superglue.

"Stand up straight when I'm talking to you, boy!" the Master shouted, as Barty, through shyness and awkwardness, leaned his hands on his desk before quickly taking up a more upright position.

"Now, Barty, just because you have snots in your nose that you can't seem to keep under control, do you think it's right that everybody else in this room needs to hear them?" the Master asked with his trademark smarm.

"No, sir," replied Barty apologetically, with his head bowed.

"And what do you think it says to me, and your fellow classmates, when you come in here and subject us all to that unbearable rattle?"

"I don't know, sir," he replied, again with his head bowed, but, this time, followed by a long and loud unintentional sniffle that led most of those in the room to break into fits of giggles.

"Look at me when I'm talking to you, boy!" the Master roared, restoring silence to the room and causing the frightened boy to lift his head and look directly towards his teacher.

"When your classmates are trying to study, it isn't very fair that you should be distracting them. You should have a think about that during lunchtime detention today! Now sit down."

"That's not fair!" interrupted a loud and relatively deep voice from the back of the classroom, as Barty resumed his seat after receiving his sentence.

"Who said that?" shouted the Master, slamming the newspaper down on his desk and rising to his feet, knowing all too well that the objection had come from Barty's older brother, Billy.

"Who said that?" repeated the Master.

All eyes in the room turned to the back corner near the window, where Billy Shanahan was seated. Billy was the oldest student in the school at thirteen years and nine months. He should have been in secondary school by this stage but, having started school a year later than convention and having repeated third class because of missing so much school time due to the untimely death of his father, Billy still found himself on the roll book of St Joseph's and in the clutches of Master Ó Luing.

Billy was the tallest and strongest boy in the school and one would have been forgiven for not realising that he and Barty were brothers, as they bore very little resemblance to each other. In contrast to his younger brother, Billy had jet-black, wavy locks and was impeccable in his dress and appearance. He was also the one student who was audacious enough to stand up to the Master and challenge his authoritarianism.

"I did," answered Billy, in a calm and collected fashion, as he rose to his feet with perfect posture, chest out, back straight and chin up.

Some of the students gasped in amazement as they awaited the Master's response to this clear display of insubordination.

"Do you think that I'm being paid to have my decisions questioned by the likes of you, Billy Shanahan?" asked the Master condescendingly.

"Considering that you have been paid by the State to do what you've been doing here for the past thirty-five years, I find it unfortunate that you're being paid at all," responded Billy calmly without even blinking an eye.

Cathal burst into laughter, momentarily losing his composure amidst the tension in the classroom. Unfortunately for him, nobody else in the room greeted Billy's response with such open enthusiasm and now the Master had another target in his sights. Not wanting to risk any further verbal jibes from the quick-witted Billy, the Master quickly dispensed justice so that he could move on from the matter. He knew that Billy was more than he could handle.

"Billy, you can join your brother in detention today, and Cathal, you'll be accompanying them. Now back to reading, and Barty, for goodness sake, go out to the bathroom and blow your nose."

Cathal couldn't believe it. Seven and a half years in his previous school and he had never been spoken to in anger by a teacher, never mind being detained at lunchtime. Less than an hour in St Joseph's and he was already in the bad books. That said, part of him felt that it was worthwhile openly condoning Billy as he socked it to the Master with such elegance, especially given what had been said by the Master outside the classroom door. Another part of him feared more and more that he was going to have a turbulent time in St Joseph's.

∼

THE LUNCHTIME BELL SOUNDED, summoning the students to the school yard for snacks and a well-earned break from academic work. Unfortunately for Cathal and the Shanahan brothers, this lunchtime would be spent in the classroom under the intermittent supervision of the Master.

When the main bulk of the students had left the classroom, only the Master and his three detainees remained behind. Rising to his feet at the top of the classroom, the Master ceremoniously dished out instructions and cautions.

"Right, I want each of you to write the following line one hundred times in your copybooks - 'I will not be a nuisance N-U-I-S-A-N-C-E in class'. If I hear any talk or noise coming from this room, even the drop of a pen, you will all be in detention tomorrow. If any one of you doesn't have the lines written correctly by the end of lunchtime, you will all be in detention tomorrow. If your handwriting is careless, you will all be in detention tomorrow. Now begin."

With that, the boys took out their copybooks and pens and started the monotonous task of writing the lines, as the Master left the room, closing the door behind him with more force than was necessary, as if to prove some point.

Immediately, the Shanahans burst into talk, with Billy accusing Barty of being the cause of their predicament.

"Nice going, Barty, you gimp, you got the three of us detention."

"It wasn't my fault," Barty squealed defensively, "I couldn't help it if my nose was running."

"Why didn't you just blow it like Auld Hairy Face suggested?"

"Shut up, right, I didn't know I was sniffling."

"Didn't know? Didn't know? There were deaf people in China who could hear you sniffling!"

"Shut up, right, none of this would have happened if you hadn't caused me to catch a cold."

Billy stared at Barty with dagger eyes.

"Shut your mouth! Shut it!" Billy insisted, as he turned his attention to Cathal to see if he was paying attention to the contents of the conversation.

By that stage, Cathal had momentarily stopped writing and had turned to observe the verbal conflict between the brothers.

"And what are you looking at?" asked Billy aggressively, making direct eye contact with Cathal.

Cathal immediately turned away and continued writing and, as he did, Barty interjected, again telling his brother to "shut up" and that "he", meaning Cathal, had "done nothing wrong". Barty and Cathal continued writing but Billy's concentration was not on his task and he turned his attention to striking up a conversation with his new classmate, although his cynical approach did not impress Cathal.

"Hi, Colin, what d'you think of Auld Hairy Face? Did he give you a good talkin' to outside the door? You looked fairly rattled when you came in."

"His name is Cathal, you clown," interrupted Barty.

"Colin, Cathal, Colm, all the same! Anyway, what'd he say to you?"

Cathal carefully weighed up the situation and figured that Billy, even though he seemed to have an intimidating manner, was still on the same side as he was when it came to Auld Hairy Face. That, and the fact that Billy was a foot taller than him and twice as strong as him, led Cathal to decide to respond in an open and friendly way.

"Not much really, just the usual. Don't cause any trouble, don't do this, don't do that. That was about it."

"That's not how it looked to me when you walked in," remarked Billy, laughing.

Cathal wasn't sure what to make of Billy; whether to laugh with him or be afraid of him, but his instinct was starting to tell him that he wasn't a bad type.

"Did he tell you that 'you're not special'?" asked Barty, as if speaking from experience.

"Yeah, he did," laughed Cathal in response and, somehow, feeling ever so slightly consoled by the realisation that this line was not conjured up by the Master especially for him.

"He always says that to me," added Barty innocently, with some joy at having someone to empathise with.

"That's because you're not, you plank," interrupted Billy.

"You're almost as bad as the Master, you are," responded Barty angrily.

"Well, at least I can see my toes without the need for a mirror," charged Billy in quick response, making clear reference to Barty's weight.

"Billy, if I get up to you, I'll kill you."

"Try it, Fatso."

That was all it took. Barty sprang to his feet, knocking his chair over with the force of the backs of his legs as he rose but, as he did, the handle of the door turned and the classroom door opened. Barty attempted to return to his original position in an instant, but with his chair now lying on the floor, a metre behind him, the boy had no choice but to squat and pretend that he was sitting at his desk as normal.

As the Master walked in, he scanned the classroom like a hawk searching for his prey. Somehow, and largely due to Barty's realistic pose, the Master didn't notice the irregularity, also failing to observe the overturned chair on the floor. The Master stood motionlessly at the top of the room, surveying the boys as the three of them diligently wrote their lines into their copybooks.

However, with every second that passed, Barty's legs were getting weaker and weaker. He felt the backs of his calves burning as he tried to hold his position but he knew that he could not hold out for much longer. He hoped that the Master wouldn't walk to the back of the room from where he would surely find him out.

The Master stayed standing at the top of the room but Barty was hurting at this stage. With the last remaining elements of resistance in his body, all the while trying to keep a straight face during his ordeal, he decided to count to ten in his head and, at ten, he was going to give up and resume a standing position or fall over, whichever would be easier.

1.
2.
3. The Master was still watching.
4.
5.
6. Still no change.
7.
8. His legs were about to collapse.
9. The Master turned for the door.
10. The Master walked out the door, closing it after him.

Barty collapsed on his rear, as Billy and Cathal burst into torrents of laughter. As soon as the immediate pain passed, Barty laughed heartily also, now lying on the flat of his back on the classroom floor. He had gotten away with it.

"Barty hasn't squatted for that long since he got caught by a call of nature the day we climbed the mountain," Billy remarked, with Barty seeing the funny side to it.

Eventually, the boys regained their composure and Barty resumed his seat at his desk.

"What time is it?" enquired Billy.

"It's 12.38pm on my watch," announced Cathal.

"That's only twenty-two minutes left. How many have ye done?" asked Billy.

"Just about to start my third one now," said Barty.

"I'm on seventeen," said Cathal.

"Swat! I'm on my first. Right, shut up lads, or we'll all be in here tomorrow. Hurry up, Barty. Don't get us all caught again."

Barty briefly considered responding to this latest jibe but decided that the requirement to complete ninety-eight lines of writing in under twenty-two minutes to avert further lunchtime detention was a more pressing matter and so started writing with determination.

The three boys didn't speak again for the remaining time, as each of them battled against the clock to complete their assignment, not out of duty, but out of a desire not to give the Master the satisfaction of imposing further sanctions on them. They concentrated on their work and, after a short while, were oblivious to the sound of their schoolmates playing noisily in the yard outside, such was the focus of their attention.

By 12.59pm exactly, as their colleagues were recalled for class by the ringing of Miss O'Shea's bell, all three boys had their hundred lines completed and ready for inspection, with Barty finishing with only seconds to spare. When the Master re-entered the room, he checked each boy's work and could find nothing to criticise them fairly on, but still could not resist commenting to each of them, "Could be neater".

Normal class resumed and Cathal discreetly looked around to Billy and Barty. Both smiled back warmly and something told Cathal then that this would not be the last sticky situation that the trio would find themselves in. He also knew that he had just made two new friends.

CHAPTER THREE

When Granda returned home after dropping Cathal to school, his first task was to see to the welfare of poor Paddy the donkey, who hadn't had as much exercise in years and who was fairly exhausted after his round trip. Granda found the best of feed that he could muster and presented it to the animal, along with a large bucket of ice-cold water from the tap in the farmyard. He gave Paddy an appreciative hug and told him he was a great donkey, with Paddy reciprocating with a big sloppy lick on Granda's face.

Granda and Paddy were the best of friends and the old man's response when quizzed on the subject was that he had no need of a dog as long as he had Paddy. After seeing that the donkey was comfortable, Granda put some tobacco in his pipe and lit it. As the smoke rose into the calm morning air, he pondered on many things.

First of all, he would have to get the car fixed. Another trip could kill poor Paddy and that wasn't a risk that Granda was willing to take. Also, although Paddy had gotten him out of a hole on that particular occasion, he wasn't a realistic long-term transportation option. He would have to give his mechanic, PJ Guerin, a call and hope that he would accept barter as a means of payment. The tractor would also have to be fixed but that could wait for a while. However, the most pressing financial burden troubling Granda was the money he owed to the loan shark that had brought the thugs to his home the previous day.

Granda knew that he had been only a very limited father and grandfather in the past, but when Cathal's father, mother and brother died, he saw it as his duty to look after the boy and do everything in his power to help him in life. In another way, he saw the circumstances as a fateful opportunity to right the shortcomings of the past, but his primary motivation was categorically to protect Cathal's best interests.

Achieving that, though, meant having to borrow money to turn his run-down and humble cottage into a place that would be acceptable as a home for his orphaned grandson. It was either that or Cathal would have to go into State care, and Granda would not let that happen.

The banks and the credit unions would not even consider his application for a loan. Michael Kavanagh, Ballycastle, had a reputation as being a rogue, albeit a lovable one, but still a rogue. To any financial institution, he was very high risk and, as a result, the old man was forced to look elsewhere for cash.

Thankfully, friends and neighbours of Cathal's parents made contributions to cover the funeral and burial expenses. The Moloneys, next door to Cathal's old home, had agreed, with the vetting and approval of the authorities, to accommodate Cathal temporarily, while Granda prepared his accommodation in Ballycastle.

A significant amount of complex legal matters remained outstanding in relation to life assurance policies and home insurance, which Cathal's parents' solicitor had informed Granda, as Cathal's guardian, would be sorted out in time. That still left Granda with a predicament as to how he would finance the home improvements and other preparations required to accommodate Cathal.

The local community welfare officer was able to come up with €500 to go towards the cost of Cathal's school uniform and schoolbooks and that was some help at least. Unfortunately, though, the county council could not provide grant aid towards the home improvements, as it was so late in the year and their budget was already spent.

To compound matters, any tradesman who came to price the improvement works would only undertake the works on the basis of cash up front. Ultimately, Granda was left with no choice but to resort to private money lenders to secure the loan that he needed, and even this was a difficult task. The first lender that Granda approached dismissed him outright, saying, "I know a bottomless pit when I see one", to which Granda replied, "I know a pitiless bottom when I see one".

After this, two further private lenders were approached. Both were sympathetic to the man's situation but neither would lend to him, even when Granda offered forty percent interest over sixty days. Granda, being too proud to approach his own friends and neighbours, who probably would have been reluctant to lend to him anyway, found himself using his Senior's Pass on the train to Dublin, early one Monday morning, in a final act of desperation. He was going to see a money lender of very questionable integrity, whose phone number he had found in a telephone box in town.

Granda met the lender in the back room of a public house, which had some very tough-looking clientele and which was located just a few minutes' walk from Heuston Railway Station. There, the deal was struck: €5,000 cash was handed over to Granda at an interest rate of forty percent in thirty days. Total repayment would be €7,000 and late-payment 'penalties' would apply.

Granda tried his best for a sixty-day repayment period, which he felt he could manage, but the lender wouldn't hear of it and Granda accepted the terms, as he had no other way of raising the cash that he needed straight away. He was to have the repayment in cash in the same room in Dublin by November 20th.

Granda didn't even know the name of the man who lent him the money, or what he looked like, as he sat behind a screen in the room where they met to strike up the deal. It was all very gangland and underworld, a far cry from the innocence and sleepiness of Ballycastle. The deadline had now passed by five days and, according to his enforcers, the lender had already increased the repayment total to €8,500.

Granda took one last puff of his pipe before quenching it and putting it back in the inside pocket of his long, brown overcoat. It was time to get to work. He locked the back door of the house behind him and then phoned PJ Guerin, explaining that there had been a small incident with his car and asking him if he would fix it for "benefits in kind".

PJ agreed and, within a half hour, had called to the house and towed the vehicle away after a brief assessment, promising to have it back by early afternoon. He asked no questions about how, where or when the damage had been done.

"No wonder they call him the best in the south-west," Granda thought.

Now it was time to assess phase one of the repayment plan. When PJ left, Granda went to the stairs where he crouched down over the bottom step. He gave the lip of the step a gentle tap and, with that, the top of the step lifted up to reveal a compartment underneath. Inside was a lone iron key, a folded sheet of paper and plenty of dust and cobwebs. Leaving the sheet of paper be, Granda took the key in his hand and replaced the lid carefully, making sure that it was safely back in the proper position.

He then proceeded to the top of the stairs, stopping at the locked door opposite Cathal's room. He put the key in the lock and, with a little jiggle, managed to turn it and unlock the door. He turned the doorknob and pushed the door, which creaked loudly as it opened, and he made a mental note to oil the hinges.

The room was in almost-total darkness, the only source of brightness being the faint light entering through the closed curtains on the far end gable window. The air was damp and musty and Granda felt the dust in his nostrils as he turned on the light and closed the door behind him. The room was lined all round with wooden shelving and it was what was on these shelves that had brought the old man in there.

Granda stood in the middle of the room and counted the units of his produce. Two hundred and forty-seven glass 700ml bottles full of the best homebrew in all of Ireland, 'Ballycastle Dew', or, as it was known to his friends, 'Mick's

Mix'. It was a few bottles less than he had remembered being there, but he figured that his memory was beginning to fail him.

He did the calculations in his head. Two hundred and forty-seven bottles minus six for PJ Guerin left two hundred and forty-one. He wanted to keep one for himself, leaving two hundred and forty for sale. At €20 per bottle, this consignment had the potential to generate €4,800. It wouldn't be enough to get the loan shark off his back, but it would form a substantial part of the debt repayment.

Mick Kavanagh was a renowned home distiller. Carrying on a centuries-old tradition in Ballycastle, he had supplemented his income for decades by providing his infamous potion to clients throughout the parish of Ballycastle and the surrounding districts. People loved it. At Christmas time, in particular, individuals would buy numerous bottles of the stuff for their own consumption, as well as for sending abroad to family and friends who had emigrated.

Over the years, he had received countless photographs of people enjoying it in various locations around the globe, including Australia, Canada, the USA and England. To those abroad, who knew the origin of their bottle, sending Mick Kavanagh a photo became a bit of a tradition in itself and some of the photos still hung in the locked room, pinned to the wooden shelves with thumbtacks that were now well rusted.

However, this batch was his final batch ever and was never meant for sale. In fact, this was his own private collection and was intended to last him for the remainder of his days.

Desperate times called for desperate measures, though, and he now knew that he would have to sell the collection. He needed to act quickly but was confident that there would be strong demand for his produce. He would have to be careful though. After all, the sale of such produce was technically against the law.

Granda turned off the light and locked the door behind him. He went back downstairs and out to the farmyard to the shed where he kept his turkeys. He looked in through the top half of the door and gazed upon the dozens of turkeys that he was fattening for Christmas. He usually killed them a few days before Christmas and sold them as fresh meat, the larger birds fetching up to €70 each. This year, he would have to kill or sell the turkeys early and settle for a reduced price by selling them as frozen turkeys or as ready to be killed.

In his head, he did more calculations - €50 multiplied by forty turkeys was €2,000. That still left him €1,700 short of his €8,500 target. He then thought of the dozen or so salmon that he had in his freezer, which he had poached from the River Clane in early autumn. They would generate another few hundred euro. Finally, he thought that if he sold three or four trailer-loads of turf from his huge private stash in his turf shed, he would have just about enough to meet the repayments, including the interest. If he fell short, for any reason, he would have to dip into his €1,000 'emergency emergency fund', which he had carefully hidden away and only ever planned to retrieve in a life-and-death situation.

He would have to sell like he never sold before and he had less than two weeks to do it, but what most people didn't know about Mick Kavanagh was that he was a very determined man when he put his mind to things, and he was determined to raise the money he needed in time to be able to go to the loan shark rather than wait for the loan shark to come to him.

～

CATHAL THOUGHT THAT 3PM would never arrive but, when it finally did, he was very glad to get out of the classroom and head for home. It had been a difficult first day in his new school but he had gotten through it and was optimistic that he was over the worst of it. As he walked towards the school gate, he scanned the entrance just to be sure that Granda and Paddy hadn't shown up to take him home. He was relieved to see that they weren't there and that the agreement that he would walk home still stood. Just as he was going out the gate, Billy Shanahan called him.

"Cathal, you going to the shop?"

"Hadn't planned to. Are ye?"

"Yeah, come on with us."

Even though the shop wasn't on Cathal's route home, it was just a short detour and given that it presented further opportunity to build on his fledgling relationship with Billy and Barty, he decided to go. After a few minutes' walking and talking about the events of the day, the three boys arrived outside the shop, which stood on its own on the side of the quiet country road.

The shop, which was a traditional two-storey building, was set back from the road just about far enough for a car, delivery van or even a tractor and small trailer to pull in and park in the rough gravel yard. There was a small wooden bench with enough seating for three or four people to the side of the front door and Cathal thought to himself that it would be a nice place to sit and watch the world go by with an ice cream on a warm summer day, but not today, in the cold of winter.

The sign above the door read 'Ballycastle Stores – Proprietor Ted Hanratty', in bold, black print, the colour scheme matching the white walls and black corner stones of the building itself. The large windows had nothing on display except old ice cream company stickers that were stuck to the glass inside the perimeters, with the colours and text having long since faded from years of exposure to sunlight.

A loud bell chimed upon opening and closing the door, following which one found oneself in a dark and pokey little store, with a strange smell that seemed to represent a cocktail of aromas from all the items for sale within the four walls. It was visibly a very old establishment. The shop unit took up most of the ground floor, with Ted Hanratty's private residence taking up the remainder of the building. On the customers' side of the counter, one could procure some of the larger items, such as peat briquettes, boxes of washing powder and bags of potatoes.

Only two modern pieces of equipment had made it into the store over the decades. One was a refrigerator for milk, cheese, ham and other perishables. The other was a large chest freezer for frozen foods and a limited selection of ice creams and ice lollies. Behind the counter, wooden shelves - filled with every item imaginable - stretched from floor to ceiling.

The trio stood at the counter, assessing the range of sweets, chocolates and fizzy drinks (not chilled) that lay on the shelves behind. After a short wait, a huge frame of a man entered the shop from an adjoining room that could only be accessed from behind the counter.

"Alright, alright, I'm coming," the boys could hear him mutter as he shuffled into the room, quenching a semi-smoked cigarette under his boot on the concrete floor as he came into view to take up position behind the counter, tying his long blue apron and fixing his capeen on his 70-plus-year-old silver head.

"Hello boys. Another day down," said Ted cheerily, realising who was there, his attention quickly shifting towards Cathal, whom he didn't recognise.

"You must be Mick Kavanagh's grandson, I suppose," remarked Ted, deducing that the new boy in the St Joseph's uniform could be none other.

"Yes, sir. Pleased to meet you."

The Shanahans laughed and Ted smiled. It seemed that such formal speak was uncommon in Ted's shop and Cathal felt a little silly.

"So how was your first day?" enquired Ted in his loud and deep voice, with a smirk that indicated that he had a fair idea that it had been challenging.

"It was - ah - interesting."

"Interesting?"

"Yes, that would best describe it, I think."

"Auld Hairy Face was up to his usual old tricks again, Ted," interrupted Billy before Barty added, "He always does that for the new kids. It's the same on the first day of every new year too".

"Jaysus, they broke the mould when they made that fella. So, ladeens, what can I get ye?"

"I'm just looking for four AAA batteries and a Mars bar, please Ted," said Billy.

"Four AAA batteries? You must be expecting a power cut," remarked Ted, as he turned towards the designated shelf for batteries.

After a little rooting and tearing, Ted produced the batteries, accepted payment and moved to his next client, Barty.

"One hundred penny sweets please, Ted," requested Barty, placing a coin on the counter.

"My dear man, I'll be here 'til tomorrow. Come in here and count them out yourself," instructed Ted, handing Barty a small brown paper bag and entrusting him with the self-regulated penny sweet compilation, which involved Barty going down on his knees to access the low shelf where the penny sweets were stored.

"And you, sir?" asked Ted, turning his attention to Cathal.

"No, I'm alright, thanks."

"What do you mean 'you're alright'? You hardly came here for nothing?" pressed Billy.

"Well, I don't have any money actually," admitted Cathal with embarrassment.

"Oh," said Billy, taken aback and sorry that he had put Cathal in such an awkward position.

"Well, it's actually tradition that new residents in Ballycastle get a free gift on their first visit here, so here you go," said Ted, handing a Mars bar to Cathal, his intervention averting any further embarrassment and showing Cathal that Ted was of a very good nature.

"Thank you very much," said Cathal, as he gladly accepted.

"You're very welcome and I am very sorry about your recent loss," added Ted, sympathetically.

"Thank you," replied Cathal sadly.

Billy broke the ensuing brief and slightly-awkward silence by turning attention to Barty, who was by now counting aloud in the mid-seventies as part of his quest to compile his century of sweets.

"Will you hurry up, Barty, for God's sake - it'll be getting dark soon."

"I'm going as fast as I can. I don't want too many of the same type. Oh, you're after making me lose count now. I'll have to start all over again."

"You were on seventy-seven so just twenty-three more," said Cathal helpfully.

"You mean thirty-three more?" a confused Barty asked.

"No, you fool. Seventy-seven and twenty-three is one hundred," added Billy, growing impatient at his brother's lack of pace and mathematical prowess.

Barty realised the arithmetic of the situation and continued carefully counting out sweets from the various containers while Billy and Cathal waited at the counter, making small talk with Ted about the weather. Barty was about to reach one hundred when a car could be heard pulling into the gravel yard outside and coming to an abrupt halt.

Within seconds, the front door burst open and closed again, with the bell almost falling off its perch, as Peggy Moore entered the shop. Automatically, Ted and the three boys each sighed loudly.

"So, I see you've found good company," said Peggy to Cathal, sarcastically referring to the Shanahans. "I hope they don't be leading you astray around the place and your poor grandfather and he trying to mind you."

Cathal was about to respond but, before he had a chance, Peggy had shifted her attention to Billy and Barty.

"Don't let me be hearing any stories coming back about how ye got this young man in trouble or I'll make sure ye'll pay for it!"

"And how would we pay then, Peggy? Cash, cheque or do you accept credit cards these days, maybe?" responded Billy spontaneously, with a broad smile across his face.

"Oh, you're a cheeky one, alright - the brains of the operation. Well, you'd have to be. You wouldn't want to be relying on Einstein behind you," she smugly replied, with a belittling downward nod towards where Barty was getting to his feet after counting out his hundredth sweet.

Barty, deeply insulted by Peggy's slur on his intellect, was desperately scouring his mind for any possible comeback that would pass as sharp, when Ted stepped in to restore calm and call Peggy to order.

"Alright, alright, that's enough now. There'll be none of that in here. Peggy, you should know a lot better at your age."

"I hope I've more sanity than that when I'm one hundred and thirteen. C'mon lads. Bye Ted," commented Billy, anxious that Peggy wouldn't have the last say, as he made for the door, with Barty and Cathal following in his wake.

He bid goodbye to Ted, who reciprocated with an apologetic expression on his face and in his voice.

"I'll be watching ye and don't be eating those sweets before yer dinner!" Peggy yelled as the boys walked away from the shop, with the door closing behind them.

"She is such an old windbag. Always has her nose stuck in everyone's business. I wish she'd just mind her own and leave us alone," complained Barty as he scoffed a handful of sweets into his mouth without breaking his stride.

"She's the neighbour from hell. There's no need for CCTV in this place with Peggy around. She doesn't miss a trick," added Billy.

Cathal, knowing by now the type that Peggy was, still could not help but wonder why she was so dismissive of the Shanahans and if there was some reason why she seemed to despise them so much. He decided he would ask.

"Why does Peggy hate the two of you so much?"

Barty and Billy looked at each other and Billy began.

"Well, it all goes back years, to when we were small lads, about six and four years old. Behind Peggy Moore's house there is a small orchard with about ten apple trees and, every autumn, those trees produce the sweetest and juiciest red apples in all of Ireland. So, it was only natural that, as young, active children, we took it upon ourselves to liberate those trees of their apples, rather than leave them for the crows to peck or to rot on the ground and be taken by rats."

Barty took over:

"So we would wait until Peggy was at Mass or gone to the shop and we'd sneak in and salvage what we could. We were getting away with it for years until about two years ago."

Billy took over again:

"It was one very hot Sunday morning and we waited in the field across the road from Peggy's house for her to leave for Mass. As soon as we heard her red Micra zoom away up the road towards the church, we hopped the ditch and legged it into her place, around to the back of the house where her orchard is. Sure enough, there were the trees, absolutely laden down with gorgeous-looking red apples. So we got our rucksacks and started filling."

Barty took up the story:

"Trouble was, there was a collection for Somalia at the church gate the same morning and when Peggy arrived at the church, she realised that she had left her purse at home. Not wanting to pass the collectors without contributing something…"

Billy interjected:

"For fear that they would be talking about her behind her back and not out of any deep ideological belief in fairness for the Third World."

Barty continued:

"Peggy decides to return home for her purse. Meanwhile, Billy is up at the top of the tallest tree in the orchard, shaking the branches like a tornado and there I am, on the ground, filling the bags with the apples as they fell."

Billy took centre stage:

"Maybe we had got complacent over the years or something, but, for some reason, we weren't as vigilant as we should have been and didn't even hear Peggy's car returning to the front of her house. Before we knew it, not only had she seen us, she actually had the presence of mind to fetch her camera and take a full series of photographs of us at work as evidence of our actions."

Barty added:

"The minute I saw her, I got the fright of my life. I shouted to Billy and took off running. Problem was, as I was trying to pull myself over the wall at the back of the orchard, the wall cap came loose and I fell onto my back, with the wall cap falling on me, giving me a nasty gash on the forehead."

Billy continued:

"The second I heard Barty warn me that she was back, I tried to get down off the tree as quickly as I could, but my foot slipped off one of the branches on the way down and I ended up falling about fifteen feet to the ground, breaking my arm when I landed on it. We both ended up in A&E and we were the laughing stock of the place."

Barty took over again:

"Worse than that, the old bag reported it to Garda O'Sullivan and took the photos with her as proof. She only agreed not to take it any further when we paid her compensation for her apples. She demanded fifty cent for every apple they found in the bags. It cost us over €50 and we never got the apples. We didn't get our rucksacks back either. She even demanded the price of printing the photographs!"

Billy finished the story:

"I wouldn't mind, but the apples were going to go waste anyway. We got awfully bad names around the place. Peggy told absolutely everyone she could tell and she still holds a grudge to this day."

Cathal laughed: "Yeah, but it was hardly the Great Train Robbery, was it? I mean - it was a few apples that were going to waste anyway. Okay, they weren't yours to take but, in fairness, it was more or less a victimless crime."

"That's the problem with Peggy Moore. She knew that and we knew that, but she couldn't resist the drama of making a big deal over nothing," sighed Barty.

By now the boys had reached the turnoff for the mountain bohereen that led to Granda's cottage and the Shanahans were continuing further along the road to their own home. Cathal bid them farewell and agreed to meet them on their way to school at 8.50am the next morning at that same point.

"Don't forget to do your homework for Auld Hairy Face," Billy yelled, as Cathal made his way uphill, looking forward to telling Granda all about the day and the encounters that he'd had.

As he reached the clearing, about one hundred metres from the cottage, he noticed that there was no smoke coming from the chimney and thought it strange that Granda would go without a fire on such a cold day. When he got to the door, he was surprised to find a note stuck to it.

Quickly snapping the note from the door, Cathal unfolded it to read what it said. In a blue ink scribble, which he assumed must be Granda's writing, the note read, 'Cathal - key of door on wheel of Plan C. Granda'. He was confused for a moment, having fully expected his grandfather to be at home when he returned from school. Now that he wasn't, Cathal realised that he needed to find the key to get into the house.

He looked again at the note and thought for a few seconds before remembering that Plan C was how he got to school that morning - the donkey and cart. If the key was anywhere, it had to be on the wheel of the cart. Cathal went straight to where the cart was parked and, sure enough, there on top of one of the wheels was the small key to the door.

When Cathal had let himself into the house, he found another note on the living room table, written in the same blue scribble. It read, 'Dear Cathal, I am terribly sorry that I had to attend to some very important business at very short notice and cannot be at home to meet you. I have left a dinner for you in the oven, to be heated in the microwave. There is loads of other stuff in the fridge if you get hungry. Be sure to do your homework and get to bed by 10pm. I may be quite late, so don't wait up. The fire is set in the fireplace, so all you have to do is put a match to it. Just be careful and keep the fireguard in place if you're not in the room. Granda'.

Cathal was immediately suspicious.

"What on earth is going on," he wondered, "why would Granda effectively abandon me on my second day living with him?"

Then he thought that maybe something more sinister was at play.

"Maybe the thugs came back and snatched Granda, forcing him to leave a note to cover their tracks and buy some time before anyone would be concerned?"

He checked the oven for the dinner that was referred to in the note and, sure enough, there, waiting for him, was a fine feed of potatoes, steak and carrots.

"This must have taken time to prepare and so the thugs could never have set all that up. The note must be genuine," he concluded.

With so many questions buzzing around in his head, Cathal decided to get stuck into his homework to try to take his mind off any niggling worries. When that was done, he heated his dinner so that mealtime would coincide with *Home and Away*. That evening's episode featured an orphan who went to live with his grandfather in Summer Bay after his entire family were wiped out in a tropical storm.

"How clichéd," Cathal thought.

After that, he had time for some more reading and a bit more television and before he knew it, it was almost 10pm. He wasn't used to having so much time by himself and, in one way, quite enjoyed the space and freedom, but thoughts of Granda and his strange absence dominated his thinking. By 10.30pm, there was still no trace of his grandfather. Cathal made sure that all of the doors were locked, the lights and electrical appliances were turned off and the fireguard was in place before he went upstairs to bed. His head was full of thoughts and ideas and theories about what was going on with Granda. He found it hard to get to sleep and was still awake when his clock radio read 11.30pm, but drifted off shortly after that.

At exactly 1.17am, the noise of an engine woke Cathal. He lay silent and vigilant in his bed, wondering what was happening and who was outside. He didn't move a muscle as he listened intently to the sound of the vehicle coming to a halt in the backyard and a handbrake being applied. After a few seconds, he heard a car door open and, a few seconds later, it closed again. It sounded as if there was only one person there.

The next thing Cathal could hear was the sound of the back door of the house opening and closing and he was slightly relieved, given that he had locked the door before he went to bed. He figured that the only way someone could have got in so quickly would be if that person had a key and the only person with a key was most likely Granda. Still, he wasn't sure and he kept thinking about the two thugs that had met him on his arrival.

He listened intently and, for about a minute, he could hear the occasional noise coming from the living room, which was directly below where his bedroom was. Cathal had just decided that he would sneak down the stairs to have a peep to be sure that it was Granda, when, as he was about to get out of bed, he heard the living room door open.

He quickly pulled his legs back in under his duvet and, as he did, he could see the glow from the landing light above the stairs, which had just been switched on and was now filtering under his bedroom door. Then he heard the footsteps coming up the stairs and prayed that it was Granda.

After a few seconds, the sound of the footsteps stopped and Cathal could see the dark shadow of a figure in the light beneath his door. Then he heard the doorknob turning and his bedroom door gently opening, just enough for someone to poke their head in to have a look in the room. Cathal was petrified.

"Good night, Cathal," whispered Granda's familiar voice after a few seconds of observation, while the boy lay motionless, pretending to be asleep.

He was so relieved when he heard his grandfather's voice. Everything seemed to be alright, but he stayed as he was, not letting Granda know that he was awake. The door closed again and Cathal sat up in his bed. He could still see the dark shadow of Granda's figure standing on the landing.

"Why is he still outside my door? Maybe he's listening to see if I'm really asleep?" he thought.

Then Cathal heard the rattling of a key in a lock and a doorknob turning and realised that Granda was at the locked door across the landing. The door squeaked open and was then closed and Cathal heard the faint sound of a light switch. After a few minutes and the odd rummaging sound, the door squeaked open once more, the light switch flicked and the door squeaked closed again.

The key rattled in the lock before Cathal heard Granda going back down the stairs. After a few seconds, the landing light went out and he heard the sound of a door closing downstairs, most likely, he thought, Granda going into his own bedroom.

Cathal was intrigued by the sequence of events: first he came home to an empty house, with very little explanation. Second, Granda arrived home in the middle of the night. Third, Granda sneaked into a locked room in the middle of the night before locking it again when he was leaving it. It was all too much for Cathal's young mind to process and, try as he might, he found himself unable to sleep.

He was restless with thought. Eventually, after tossing and turning for what seemed like an eternity, Cathal sat up in his bed again: 3.42am was the time on his clock radio. He thought that maybe a brief amble around the room and a stretch of his limbs might help him settle. He switched on his bedside lamp, quietly got out of bed and walked towards the window of his room where he put his head between the curtains to have a look out.

It was pitch dark outside and Cathal wondered if he switched his light off whether he would be able to see the stars. He quickly did just that and returned to the window to look skyward. After a few minutes, when his eyes had fully adjusted, he realised that he wouldn't be seeing any stars that night, given the heavy cloud that seemed to be stationary overhead.

The countryside was in darkness, with only the street lights of Killcrown visible across the harbour, glowing a hazy orange. Just then, he thought he saw a flash of light in the general area where he thought Ballycastle Pier was. He looked again, cautious that his weary eyes and mind might be playing tricks on him and, sure enough, after a few seconds, there was the light again, which disappeared after about five seconds. Cathal was mystified. The light was too dim to be that of a car or any other vehicle.

He wondered who on earth would be out at this hour. He looked again but couldn't see anything. Then, after about a minute, it appeared again. By now, it was some distance from where he had first seen it and moving very slowly, as if at walking pace, for a few seconds more before disappearing again. He watched and waited to see if the light would reappear, but there was no sign of it anymore.

Cathal got back into bed, physically and mentally spent, but putting together a line of questioning for Granda in the morning. Finally, exhaustion overcame the activity in his mind and he fell asleep.

CHAPTER FOUR

It was Tuesday morning, usually Cathal's least favourite day of the week. Tuesday mornings meant that there were four full days of school until the weekend and very little news to catch up on, because most of it had been shared on Monday morning. However, on this particular morning, Cathal jumped out of bed and was downstairs and at the breakfast table in record time.

He didn't want to waste a minute that he might use to question Granda on various topics such as his absence the previous evening, the locked room and the strange light. He also wanted to tell him all about his encounter with the Master, his meeting with Ted Hanratty, the run-in with Peggy Moore, and his friendship with the Shanahans.

Granda was sitting at his usual place at the table, finishing a large bowl of porridge and sipping tea from his mug. Cathal fetched his share of porridge from the saucepan that sat on the cooker, steam still rising from it as he poured it into his bowl. After some small talk, Granda pre-empted Cathal's first question by taking the initiative to explain his whereabouts on the previous day.

"Cathal, I'm so sorry that I wasn't here yesterday when you got home from school. After PJ Guerin dropped the car back to me at 2pm, I had some important paperwork to take care of at the solicitor's office in town. After that, I had to call to a friend of mine, who's in hospital. On the way home, I had another visit to make. Before I knew it, it was after midnight."

Cathal wasn't sure if the old man was telling the full truth, half the truth or if the account was a total fabrication, but it just wouldn't have been appropriate for him to pry, under the circumstances, without appearing openly suspicious. He was anxious not to come across as rude or cheeky in any way and therefore asked no questions. Even if he wanted to, Granda quickly moved the conversation on to the next topic.

"So, how was your first day at school?"

Cathal told him all about his day, although not revealing the extent of the Master's nastiness. Granda listened to every word, delighted by his grandson's enthusiasm for the new world that he found himself in. They both mocked the Master and his ways and Peggy Moore and her nosiness, while agreeing that Ted Hanratty was one of life's true gentlemen.

Granda was delighted to hear about the rapport that Cathal had built up with the Shanahans, knowing that if he was to be happy in his new school, it would help to make new friends. Then Cathal decided to tell Granda about the mysterious light that he had seen from his bedroom window, telling a little white lie when he said that he had gone to the window for some fresh air, having been woken by the heat of his super-cosy bedroom. Granda was enthralled with the story.

"My God, you're after seeing Seánín Solas!"

"Seánín Solas?"

"Yes, Seánín Solas!"

"Who on earth or what in the world is Seánín Solas?" Granda looked at the clock. It was 8.35am.

"No, I'll tell you another time. I wouldn't have enough time now."

"No, Granda, tell me, tell me. I'm not meeting the Shanahans 'til ten to at the bottom of the road so we've got ten minutes before I have to leave. Please, Granda."

"Alright so, although if I was to tell it right, I'd want a full hour."

Granda sat upright in his chair, moving his empty bowl aside and pulling his mug of tea closer to him. Cathal sat enthusiastically opposite him, his empty porridge bowl also moved aside, with both his hands wrapped around his own mug of tea, eagerly waiting for the story. Granda began.

"Seánín O'Connor worked for many decades at Murphy's Estate, which is in the middle of the woods on the opposite bank of the River Clane, just beyond Killcrown Pier. I pointed it out to you from the window here on Sunday when you arrived. Anyway, Seánín was employed by the Murphy family as a caretaker, gardener and general security man on the estate and woods.

"He was a strange type of a man, who lived alone in a small cottage on the grounds of the estate and never really mixed much with any of the locals. That said, he was never any trouble to anyone. Anyone, that is, except people who were trespassing in the estate and woods.

"Seánín took great pride in keeping the place in good condition, making sure all the trees and shrubs were as they should be and that all the ditches and dykes were cleared and neat, with the barbed wire fences properly intact around the perimeter of Murphy's land. He loved trees and would plant new ones every chance he got. There are loads of different varieties of trees in those woods because of him.

"Anyhow, sometimes, around Christmas time, some of the locals would try to sneak into the forest at nighttime and steal some of the pine trees to use them as Christmas trees. The first time it happened, about fifty years ago, two men from Killcrown came, under the cover of darkness, and chopped down a tree each to take home to their families.

"Seánín was devastated on realising what had happened when he discovered the tree stumps the following morning. It was as if he had lost family members. He was in a state of near-mourning. People used to say that the trees were his family, since he had none of his own. Then, it happened again a few nights later, when three more trees were cut down by different men who heard about where you could get free Christmas trees.

"Seánín's sadness quickly turned to anger. He was furious that people would cut down his precious trees and was even more furious with himself for not preventing it, not just once, but twice. He made a promise to himself and to the trees that he would do everything in his power from that moment on to protect the trees from the hands of 'murderers'.

"His first victim came along that very night. A friend of the men who cut the other trees decided he would have a tree for himself. After leaving one of the pubs in Killcrown, and it being a fine, still night, he walked down the road towards the estate in the moonlight and crossed the barbed wire fence that separated the woods from the road.

"What he didn't realise was that Seánín was on the lookout that night. When the intruder found the tree he wanted, he took a small hatchet to the bark of the tree and started chopping. As soon as Seánín heard the hatchet hitting the bark, he ran towards where the intruder was, carrying his torch and a shotgun. As soon as Seánín saw the intruder in the distance, he discharged a shot from the gun into the air.

"The intruder got the shock of his life and, by now, he could see the light coming towards him through the trees. He dropped his hatchet on the spot and took off, running away from the light. By now, though, a thick layer of cloud had covered the moon and the intruder lost all sense of direction in the darkness, was scared out of his wits and was half drunk after having been in the pub earlier.

"What happened next is unclear but it is thought that Seánín discharged shot after shot into the air and the unfortunate intruder went near insane with fear, thinking that he was being directly fired at. In his desperate efforts to escape the gunfire, he ran away at top speed but, in the darkness and with all the confusion, the poor soul ran straight into a big tree trunk, causing himself a serious head injury. This only made him more confused and the poor man got back on his feet and took off again, even faster than before, in a different direction. Alas, the same thing happened again and again and again, his head taking an awful blow every time. Finally, when he had almost reached safety, he ran straight into the barbed wire perimeter fence, suffering terrible cuts and fatally wounding himself in the process.

"When his body was found in the morning, they say the look of terror on his face was enough to frighten even the most hardened of souls, and that the Garda who found him was never the same again."

"Oh my God! That's desperate, Granda," gasped Cathal, wide-eyed in disbelief, his hand covering his mouth with the shock of it.

"But that's not all," said Granda. "Even here in Ballycastle, across the River Clane, people were woken from their sleep by the dying man's screams in the still of that dreadful night."

"Oh Granda, why did you tell me that story?"

"Well, you were the one who insisted on hearing it. Now, on to the second victim."

"No, no, no, no, no, no, Granda, I don't want to hear anymore. That's enough," exclaimed Cathal.

"Are you sure, boy? Because the next victim was even more interesting."

"No, I'm sure, Granda. I'm sure. That's enough."

"Okay so. Well, to cut a long story short, what you probably saw last night was Seánín Solas, as he has come to be known, *solas* being the Irish word for light, out patrolling his woods, keeping the intruders out as Christmas comes near."

"But, if that was fifty years ago, he must be really old now, Granda."

"Old? My dear boy," Granda smiled, "Seánín Solas has been dead with the last twenty years. What you saw last night was his ghost. Now, look at the time. It's a quarter to nine. You don't want to be late to meet the Shanahans. Away with you!"

Granda rose from his seat and gathered the empty mugs and bowls while Cathal, still in a state of amazement after the story he had just heard, put on his coat and picked up his schoolbag.

"See you this evening, Granda," he said as he headed through the door.

"Have a good day, Cathal. I'll be here waiting."

Cathal quickened his pace to a jog as soon as he left Granda's yard, the fall of ground assisting him along the way, with the cool morning air filling his lungs and clearing his nostrils as he went.

"Have I really seen a ghost, albeit from a few kilometres' distance? Did Granda's story really happen? Are those woods really haunted?" Cathal asked himself question after question.

For one who would normally embrace stories of hauntings, ghosts and the supernatural, this was all just a tad too real for Cathal and he felt rather uneasy about the whole thing. He looked at his watch. It was 8.50am exactly as he arrived at the bottom of the bohereen, just in time to meet the Shanahans. Except that the brothers were nowhere to be seen. 8.55am came and went and Cathal was growing more than anxious, with class starting at 9.10am.

At 9am exactly, tired of waiting and under pressure to get to class on time, Cathal ran as fast as he could to school. He made it just in time and was sitting at his desk with only seconds to spare before the Master walked into the classroom. As they all stood to recite the Morning Prayer, Cathal looked around and noticed Billy and Barty's seats were empty. He wondered why they weren't at school and where they could be.

∼

THE ELEVEN O'CLOCK BREAK ARRIVED following an hour of supervised reading and fifty minutes of algebra instruction, delivered in the most uninteresting and monotonous manner in the history of education by the Master. Cathal was very nervous about breaktime, given that the Shanahans were absent and he hadn't spoken to anyone else in the school. Everyone in the yard gathered in pairs or groups, but Cathal was all alone, trying desperately not to be noticed.

At one stage, he saw a group of girls from his class huddled together looking in his direction and giggling as soon as he glanced their way. He walked around the back of the school, where he thought it would be quieter and where he might be 'comfortably' alone until the bell rang. He wouldn't be alone for too long, though.

Thump! A fist struck the back of Cathal's head and the blow almost knocked him off balance. Unbeknownst to him, as soon as he had turned the corner at the gable end of the school, a group of five of the fifth class boys, led by Ivan O'Toole, had followed him. Ivan had dispensed the punch as a very hostile 'welcome to St Joseph's'.

Cathal turned to face him, the other boys laughing as they bunched in behind Ivan, who was taller and stronger than Cathal, even though he was only in fifth class. He had tightly-cut black hair, pale white skin and piercing eyes and was the ultimate school bully.

"You wanna fight, townie boy?" Ivan goaded, his fists clenched and held up in a boxing position, while the boys behind pushed him forward and encouraged him with lines such as "Go on, Ivan" or "Get him, Ivan" and even "Kill him,

Ivan". Cathal didn't respond, frozen to the spot, outnumbered and feeling hopeless.

"What's wrong with you, orphan boy? Can't talk?" Ivan added, trying to provoke retaliation from Cathal, the other boys laughing and jeering all the while.

Cathal didn't know what to do. Ivan pushed him in the chest and Cathal fell on the ground. He got up quickly, but no sooner was he back on his feet than he was down on the ground again with Ivan standing over him shouting, "Get up and fight", while the others continued to laugh and jeer. Cathal was deciding whether to stay on the ground and save himself another fall or get up and try to salvage what little dignity he had left, when Miss O'Shea's bell to reconvene classes was heard ringing at the front of the school.

"Saved by the bell, townie," Ivan sneered, "but I'll get you at lunchtime," he added as he turned to walk away.

Cathal was shaking with shock on the ground and he felt totally humiliated. He waited for a few moments to try to regain his composure before brushing himself off and going around to the front of the school, from where all of the others had already gone back inside. This was just what he didn't need. All of a sudden, putting up with the Master seemed a doddle compared to the violence of the school yard. In just under eighty-five minutes, it would be lunchtime and he would have to face Ivan and his gang again, all by himself. He didn't stand a chance.

He thought of telling the Master, but dismissed the idea immediately. He then thought that maybe he could tell Miss O'Shea but felt that he'd be known forevermore as a coward if he did that. Cathal made the mistake of bottling it up and waiting for lunchtime. As he sat in class, the clock's hands moving all the while closer to 12.30pm, he pondered his fate. Then he came up with an idea.

"I've got it," he thought, "detention! It's the only thing that will save my bacon."

He would be deliberately disruptive, disrespectful or whatever it took to have his lunchtime liberty withdrawn by the Master.

"Surely, if I got detention yesterday for the slightest misdemeanour, getting it today through deliberate action should be no problem," he told himself.

Cathal wasted no time in putting his plan to work. While the Master was giving a geography and politics lesson on the main differences between North Korea and South Korea, Cathal left out a loud yawn, accompanied by a protracted stretch, as he would do if at home, sitting on the armchair watching television. Some of the class giggled and the Master stopped the lesson immediately, moving his glasses to the tip of his nose and peering at Cathal from the top of the room.

"Here we go," thought Cathal smugly, "that should do the trick."

"Cathal Kavanagh," said the Master, "Two hundred lines tonight for homework – 'I will not yawn and stretch in class.'"

"What?" gasped Cathal in amazement, certain that he had done enough to earn lunchtime detention.

"Make that three hundred," added the Master, topping up the penalty on account of the verbal protestation.

Cathal was disgusted. Not only was he still on course to get a thumping at lunchtime but he was going to have to spend the night writing lines with whichever of his fingers remained unbroken. The Master was now on to the Korean War and discussing the importance of the 38th parallel when Cathal thought about how Barty had earned his place in detention the previous day.

After a few minutes of the loudest and most deliberate sniffling that Cathal had ever performed, he finally caught the Master's attention, who - once again - stopped the lesson to reprimand him.

"Cathal, go out to the bathroom and blow your nose. Don't be a pig."

The Master continued with the lesson, as Cathal left the room for a few moments, not believing that the Master had skipped an opportunity to punish him, opting to refer to him as a pig instead.

"What do I have to do?" he wondered.

As Cathal was returning to the classroom after a few moments of doing nothing in the bathroom, he couldn't help but glance towards where Ivan O'Toole was sitting. Ivan was staring back at him and followed him with his eyes to his seat. Cathal felt extremely intimidated.

Time continued to tick by and he was still a free man for lunchtime. The Master was by now on one of his many tangents, giving a detailed account of the first lunar landing, when Cathal thought it necessary to step things up a gear.

Bang! Cathal's chair fell against the desk behind him and he fell theatrically off it in a way that could never have happened accidentally.

"This will surely do the trick," he thought.

"Stand up, Cathal," instructed the Master. "You can stay standing for the rest of the day if you can't stay on your seat."

Some of the class chuckled, as Cathal got to his feet. He was finding it hard to believe that the Master had failed to sentence him with his favourite punishment method, detention, after having committed three offences that would each normally earn such a penalty.

It was now 12.15pm and Cathal, still standing at his desk, had all but given up hope of earning lunchtime detention when a knock came to the classroom door.

"Come in," said the Master, following which the door slowly opened and Billy and Barty Shanahan strolled sheepishly into the classroom.

Cathal couldn't believe his luck; he was saved. He would have protection at lunchtime and there would be no beating now that the Shanahans would be there to row in with him. He turned towards Ivan O'Toole with a broad smile of satisfaction across his face.

"Where were you two all morning?" asked the Master, rising to his feet at the top of the room and staring straight at the Shanahans.

"I'm sorry, sir, we slept in," replied Billy, to the amusement of his classmates, as he took his seat at the back of the classroom.

"You're over three hours late. That's a long time to sleep in. We'd all like to sleep in until noon every day but some of us take our responsibilities seriously. You can have a think about that during lunchtime detention."

Billy and Barty bowed their heads in defeat, while Cathal felt a weakness at his knees. He was back to square one again and, as he glanced over at Ivan O'Toole, he saw him smirk before running his index finger across the front of his throat in that age-old threatening gesture.

"This is going to be horrific," Cathal thought, as the clock struck 12.30pm.

～

Granda went upstairs to the locked room as soon as Cathal had left for school. He reached up high to one of the top shelves and brought down a small, wooden cigar box. He slid it open, revealing a wad of banknotes inside. Taking the notes out, Granda began to count. €2,480 was the sum he reached after two careful counts. Then, counting the number of bottles remaining on the shelves, Granda reached a figure of one hundred and sixteen. The stock-take matched the turnover. He had sold one hundred and twenty-four bottles on the previous evening and night, which was all he could safely conceal in his car.

Better still, he had taken orders for seventy more bottles while out on the road. Some of his clients, so delighted to have one more chance to avail of his famous beverage, ordered by case-loads of twelve bottles each. One publican, eager for a long-lasting supply of Ballycastle Dew for under-the-counter sales to his regular customers, ordered three full cases. Thirty-six bottles sold to one customer netted a windfall of €720 for Granda and he even got a complimentary glass of stout for his troubles.

Another client, who bought just one bottle, wanted it as a rub-on muscle warmer for his racing greyhound. One old friend of Granda's took two bottles, claiming that a small measure of it mixed with boiling water and a spoon of honey was the best cure known to man for the common cold.

Granda planned to deliver the seventy pre-ordered bottles without delay and find homes for the forty-six remaining unsold bottles. He estimated that he would be back to his little cottage before 3pm to meet Cathal on his return from school. He reversed his old Carina up to the back door of the house and loaded up the boot with the remaining one hundred and sixteen bottles, using some second-hand cardboard boxes as cases. His precious cargo loaded, Granda set off on his journey.

A few minutes after leaving home, on approaching Ballycastle village, Granda was forced to come to a halt. Peggy Moore, out for her usual morning walk and gossip reconnaissance mission, was strategically sauntering along in the middle of the road, effectively forcing Granda to stop, as the road was too narrow for him to drive around her.

Her plan having worked, Peggy went to the driver's side window, tapping for him to unwind the glass for the interrogation to begin, her hand resting on the roof of the car as if placing it there would keep Granda for as long as she wanted to keep him.

"Where are you off to, Mick Kavanagh?"

"Just going for a drive, Peggy."

"Going for a drive on a Tuesday morning? All by yourself and your best attire on you? I'd say you have some business to attend to."

"Well, maybe a small bit of business too, Peggy."

"I partly guessed you were up to something. What business would that be exactly?"

"Nothing that would interest you too much, Peggy."

Peggy paused for a moment, staring at Granda as if acknowledging that he wouldn't be giving her much information. She began an alternative line of questioning.

"I see PJ Guerin was up to you yesterday morning. Took the car away on his recovery truck and dropped it back to you again around 2pm."

"Oh, I'd say it was closer to 2.05pm, Peggy," said Granda sarcastically.

"Well, whatever time it was, there can't have been that much wrong with it if he had it fixed in a few hours, although as it passed me on the road, I could have sworn that one of the windows was broken. Then again, my eyesight isn't the best. I can't see very well anymore."

"I'm sure your eyesight is just fine, Peggy."

"You were late getting home last night, Mick. I could have sworn I saw your car passing at around one o'clock in the morning."

Granda pretended to ignore the comment, privately wondering if there was anything that happened in Ballycastle that Peggy Moore didn't know about.

"So, any other news around the place, Peggy?" asked Granda, changing the subject.

"I see your young grandson has fallen in with the wrong crowd already. It didn't take him long to get involved with those little thieves, the Shanahans. In Hanratty's he was with them after school yesterday evening, Mick. I'd keep a close eye on that if I were you."

"I'm sure Cathal is well capable of choosing his own friends, Peggy."

"That's the problem, a boy of that age is easily led astray and, before you know it, you'll have a criminal drug addict on your hands."

Granda threw his eyes up to heaven as Peggy took a step back to observe the rear end of his car, which was clearly weighed down from the weight of the bottles in the boot.

"What's in the boot, Mick?"

"Ah nothing, Peggy," replied Granda nervously, "I'm just, ah, taking a few bits and pieces to the dump."

"Oh, right, it must be a few heavy bits and pieces."

Granda, all the while anxious to proceed, had put the car into gear with his foot on the clutch and had released the handbrake, but Peggy still didn't get the message and kept talking, her hand resting on the roof of the car once again. As she incessantly ranted on about the youth of today and how they had lost all respect and manners, Garda Jim O'Sullivan approached in the Garda patrol car on his way from the village.

Granda's car, still stationary in the middle of the road, was blocking his path and the Garda's car came to a halt to allow the old man to move aside. When Granda had pulled over to allow room to pass, Garda O'Sullivan stopped again as he came alongside the car and rolled down his window.

Granda prayed that it had nothing to do with his recently re-established bootlegging business. If the bottles in his boot were found, they would surely be confiscated and he would be over €2,000 out of pocket, unable to pay the loan shark and facing a day in court.

"Good morning Mick, good morning Peggy."

"Ah, good morning Jim," both replied. "Nice morning, Jim," Granda added calmly.

"It is for sure, Mick," the Garda agreed. "How's our new resident settling in?"

"Oh, he's grand out, Jim. Enjoying school and making new friends."

"He's fallen in with those Shanahans, Jim," Peggy interrupted. "You should keep an eye on them. They'll be up to no good."

"I'm sure he'll be just fine, Peggy," said the Garda. "I hope he'll be happy here, Mick."

"Thank you, Jim. I'll do my best for him anyway."

"I've no doubt you will. By the way, Mick, I'd be very careful if I were you."

Granda became very tense. Peggy took a step back.

"Why so is that, Jim?" said Granda.

"That load in the boot of your car," the Garda said, pointing to the depressed wheel arches.

Granda gulped.

"Yes?"

"I'd be very slow going through the village because there's a massive pothole just outside McCarthy's Bar and if you hit it with that load, you'll burst a shock or a spring or something."

"Oh, right. Thanks Jim," Granda replied with relief. "I'll remember that. Okay, I'd better be off now, I'm on a tight schedule."

With that, Granda took off swiftly, leaving a thick cloud of smoke from his exhaust, desperate to escape the awkward situation that he had just found himself in and perhaps appearing just a bit suspicious given the haste in which he departed.

As he looked in his rearview mirror, he could see Peggy Moore leaning in the window of the squad car, no doubt imparting some piece of vital espionage to the local Garda, who was always happy to gather information from her, no matter how trivial or insignificant. Granda hoped that it had nothing to do with him and, for a few miles, kept checking his rearview mirror in case the Garda was in pursuit. After a while, his paranoia eased as he realised that he had gotten away with it.

Granda's route took him to every pocket of the county, delivering all seventy of the pre-ordered bottles and making new sales along the way. The demand was more than he could ever have anticipated and, by 2pm, he had sold his last bottle to a woman who would be sending it to her son in Japan for him to enjoy over Christmas.

In just a day and a half, he had cleared all of his collection of Ballycastle Dew and had generated just under €5,000 to go towards his debt repayment.

He would be back to his little cottage, with his money safely hidden away upstairs, just in time to welcome Cathal home from his second day at school and to close another deal that he had struck while out on the road.

CHAPTER FIVE

"Lunchtime! All out," cried the Master. "Get some fresh air into your lungs. Except for you, Billy and Barty. Ye were getting plenty of fresh air while everyone else was at school."

The Master left the classroom, with the students streaming after him. Ivan O'Toole and his disciples were first out to the school yard, eagerly anticipating the showdown with the 'townie'. Cathal delayed at his desk until the others had left the room before engaging with the Shanahans.

"I'm in serious trouble guys," he exclaimed in a panic, "Ivan O'Toole and his mates are going to give me a hiding when I go outside."

"Calm down, calm down," said Billy. "What the heck is goin' on?"

"I don't know but, for some reason, Ivan O'Toole's after taking a major dislike to me. They ganged up on me around at the back during eleven o'clock break and now they want to finish the job."

Cathal barely had the words spoken when the Master returned to the room and, on seeing Cathal, instantly ordered him out of the room. The Master closed the classroom door as Cathal left, before beginning to administer a telling-off to the Shanahans.

"Here I go - dead man walking," Cathal thought, as he slowly stepped out into the yard.

Ivan and most of his gang were by now waiting at the back of the school, well out of the view of Miss O'Shea, who was supervising all that was happening in the main playing area. Two of the fifth class boys, Johnny Kelliher and Richie O'Brien, had remained at the school door, awaiting Cathal's emergence.

"Ivan wants to talk to you around the back," said Johnny.

"He wants to have a chat with you. He won't hurt you," added Richie.

Cathal looked the two of them straight in the eyes, thinking what fools they must be to think that he might believe them.

"I'm going up there now," Cathal replied, resigned to his destiny.

He slowly walked towards the back of the school, with Johnny and Richie running ahead of him to announce his imminent arrival. Meanwhile, in the classroom, the Master was delivering a lengthy and spit-ridden lecture to the Shanahans on the importance of punctuality, respect for fellow classmates and the dangers of school absenteeism.

It was a speech that they had both heard umpteen times before, as the Master used the same material every time. He was approaching the part where he usually delivered sentencing of a few hundred lines or an essay about some abstract topic (the most recent title given to Barty was 'The

Hopes and Aspirations of a Falling Leaf'), when a girl from the junior infants class ran into the room.

"Master! Master! There's a tourist from America or England or someplace and he's at the school gate and he's looking to see where his Nana used to live and all his old family and he wants to go in the right direction and I told him that you know everything and I said I'd go get you and he's waiting outside for you," reported the little girl breathlessly, the occasion to address the Master being the high point of her week.

"Oh, is there? Well, I had better get out there and meet this man so, and thank you very much for letting me know, Laura," replied the Master, smiling and bending down to the little girl's level.

He spoke to her in such sweet tones that it almost made the Shanahan brothers vomit. Billy thought it pathetic how it massaged the Master's ego to hear a five-year-old declare that he knew everything and now he had a chance to impress upon a tourist his version of local history and genealogy.

"Not a word out of you two," growled the Master to the boys, leaving the room in such a hurry that he forgot to announce their punishment.

Barty sprang to his feet and went to the door to watch as the Master walked down the corridor and out to the school yard.

"Come on Billy, we might have time yet," cried Barty, running out of the classroom, with his brother following close behind.

The Shanahans poked their heads out the main door of the school and saw the Master engrossed in deep conversation with the tourist at the gate, his hands pointing in various directions towards the surrounding countryside as he dispensed information by the shovel-load.

"Let's go. He's not going to see us," said Barty, taking off in a sprint towards the back of the school, with Billy quickly overtaking him en route.

The Shanahans arrived at the fight scene just as Ivan had caught Cathal in a headlock, with the other fifth class boys and some onlookers cheering and encouraging more violence. Poor Cathal was no match for Ivan, who smiled to his gang the more Cathal struggled.

"Let him go now," shouted Billy with authority, the cheering coming to an abrupt halt as he broke his way through the ring of spectators to where the protagonists were entangled.

Cathal's face had by then turned bright red from the strain of trying to shake off his bigger and stronger attacker. Ivan, knowing that he was no match for Billy, who was by far the biggest and strongest boy in the school, released Cathal from the headlock at once and stood facing the approaching Billy with an expression of guilt and fear on his face.

Cathal, through the trauma and stress of the moment, had lost awareness of what was going on around him and hadn't realised that Billy was just after intervening, so, as soon as he felt himself wriggle free, he closed his fist and caught Ivan - with all the strength he could muster - with a right hook directly under the nose.

The spectators gasped as Ivan fell flat on his back, his nose and upper lip spouting blood over his pale skin. Cathal stood over Ivan in disbelief at his own fighting ability, his fists still clinched, vigilantly looking all around in case anyone else might try to attack him.

"Anyone else want a punch?" Cathal shouted at the crowd, as he turned three hundred and sixty degrees, offering a fight to anyone who wanted it, the adrenalin pumping through his body, a feeling of invincibility having overtaken him.

The spectators all stepped back from Cathal, and Ivan's gang hurriedly dispersed without anything further to say for themselves. Still on the ground, Ivan sat up with his hands to his nose, the blood flowing from his lip and nostrils. Then Cathal noticed that Billy was standing next to him.

"Billy, you just missed it. I decked him," Cathal cried aloud with euphoria.

"I just caught the end of it, Cathal," replied Billy, trying to remain serious and not wanting to tarnish Cathal's interpretation of his victory.

Barty laughed.

"I saw it Cathal. He didn't stand a chance against you."

"I know," replied Cathal, "I didn't know I was capable of that."

By now, Ivan had risen to his feet and was stumbling away towards the main school yard. He looked back at Cathal, as if to leave a parting threat but, seeing the blood on his hands and uniform and noting that he was all alone, he realised that he had been defeated, and walked away with his head hanging. He couldn't believe how he had just been humiliated in front of all of his gang.

The Shanahans, their work complete, sneaked back into the classroom, their excursion unnoticed by the Master, who was still entertaining the tourist at the school gate. Cathal spent the remainder of the lunchbreak strutting around the school yard with a spring in his step, his confidence at an all-time personal high and feeling that nobody would ever mess with him again during his time at St Joseph's. When class resumed, the Master asked Ivan what had happened to his face, which by then had stopped bleeding but was clearly marked.

"I fell, sir," was his reply after a short delay, his head bowed, his ego bruised much more than any part of his body.

∼

WHEN CATHAL ARRIVED HOME, a lorry was in the backyard and Granda was receiving money from the driver. Cathal could hear the ear-splitting racket of gobbling turkeys coming from inside the lorry. Granda had sold his Christmas turkeys early, for €35 each, generating just €1,400, which was €600 less than he had budgeted for and half what they would have fetched had he killed them himself to sell fresh for Christmas. Still, as he saw it, it was cash up front and there was no nasty business involving having to kill the turkeys himself, a job he never liked doing.

Cathal said nothing about events in the school yard. He thought it best not to tell in case it would worry his grandfather in any way. Drained from two nights of broken sleep, an energy-sapping fight and half a school day standing at his desk, Cathal went to bed earlier that night than he had done for years, just before the *Nine O'Clock News*. He slept soundly for about six hours but woke just after 3am, his body clock out of kilter and unable to get back to sleep.

Lying in his bed, he could see the moonlight through the curtains. His mind was buzzing as he thought about his action-packed second day in St Joseph's, still unable to believe that he had really managed to defend himself against the school bully. He remembered his parents and his brother and reflected on how much he missed them all. He wondered about Granda, the money he owed, the thugs and what was in the locked room across the landing.

Then he remembered the story of Seánín Solas and the phantom light and wondered if it really was a true story. The more he analysed and considered the story, the more his curiosity grew about the light. After considerable hesitation, Cathal decided that he would take a look out his window to see if Seánin Solas or the phantom light, or whatever it was, could be seen again.

Opening the curtains just wide enough to peer out, Cathal was amazed by the size and brightness of the moon that night. The countryside all around the cottage was illuminated in bright grey light and he could clearly make out the fields, trees, houses and other features of the landscape, near and far. Most spectacular of all was the reflection of the moonlight on the river and harbour, their tranquil waters glistening and sparkling.

All along the middle of the waterway, a narrow silver corridor stretched for miles, parallel to the banks and shorelines. This was one of the most beautiful sights that Cathal had ever seen and he thought to himself how lucky he was to live in such a beautiful part of the world. For a few moments, he forgot the real purpose of his actions. Then, remembering what he was looking for, Cathal scanned the general area where he had seen the light the previous night but there was nothing.

He waited and waited but no light could be seen. He could faintly make out Killcrown Pier on the far side of the River Clane, with Murphy's Woods just a short distance beyond. Further away, the orange lights of the town of Killcrown were clearly visible. On the near side of the river, Ballycastle Pier was just about discernible. The relatively narrow waterway between both piers was lit exquisitely by the moon.

Cathal's gaze was captured by the beautiful sight, the result of collusion between man and nature. It was during this time that he noticed a black shadow on the water on the far side of the river, just out from Killcrown Pier. He watched closely as the shadow moved further away from the pier towards the Ballycastle side of the river. As it came closer and became totally surrounded by the backdrop of the glistening water, Cathal recognised the shadow to be a small boat. He looked on in astonishment, wondering what was going on.

He observed as the boat came all the way to Ballycastle Pier on the near side of the river. He watched as closely as he could, trying hard the whole time not to blink, for fear of missing some development. However, after the boat reached Ballycastle Pier, it and the occupants disappeared from view and weren't seen again that night by Cathal.

After about an hour of further close observation, he closed his curtains and lay back into bed, having grown tired of seeing nothing more by the river bank. By now, though, his curiosity had been roused beyond the point of no return. Something strange was going on every night down near the water and Cathal was determined to find out what was happening. He made a resolution to himself as he drifted off to sleep that he would investigate matters up close the following night.

~

Wednesday, November 27th - Cathal's third day at his new school - was a relatively uneventful day at St Joseph's. One of the main highlights was Barty falling asleep at his desk and breaking wind loudly as he slept, which had the classroom in raptures but incurred the wrath of the Master, who mercilessly sentenced Barty to lunchtime detention for the third day in a row. The class learned a poem about the River Clane, which Cathal found interesting, especially given that he would be paying it a visit later that night.

At the end of the school day, Cathal didn't wait around for Billy and Barty. As soon as the signal to go was given, he was first out of the classroom and ran all the way to Ted Hanratty's. There, he bought himself a new pair of wellington boots and a torch with batteries. He had the items stuffed into his schoolbag just before the Shanahans arrived in the shop.

"You were in a fierce hurry this evening," Billy said, surprised that Cathal hadn't waited for them.

"Sorry guys, I'm in a bit of a rush to get home and help Granda on the farm before it gets dark," Cathal lied.

"Oh, right," said Barty, "I didn't think you were the farming type. I suppose it's never too late to learn."

"I'll wait for ye now, though, if ye're heading home too," Cathal added.

Barty and Billy made their purchases and joined Cathal on the walk home. Barty had his usual hundred sweets and

Billy bought a twelve-metre length of nylon rope, which Cathal found a little perplexing. Cathal considered telling the brothers about the mysterious light and boat that he had seen but decided against this, fearing that his new friends might think him odd or melodramatic. They parted company at the usual location and agreed to meet there again in the morning.

Later that night, when Cathal had completed his homework, he sat down for a good chat with Granda before bedtime. They discussed everything, from school to farming to the price of turkeys. Cathal recited his poem, 'Ancient River Clane', which he had learned by heart.

Ancient River Clane

Your waters lap against your shore
As they have done for years before
The cool autumnal breeze that follows
Chases away the ling'ring swallows.
The sun and moon are changing shifts
While from your vein a salmon lifts.
The golden reed-heads dance and shift.
Your sweet aromas set adrift.

Though your body may set sail,
Eternally your soul remains.
Your new blood breathes life after rain,
Your grateful clan you will sustain.
My soul will walk with you again
Oh awesome ancient River Clane.

Granda remarked, with tears in his eyes, on how he remembered Cathal's father standing in front of the very same fireplace, reciting that very same poem, years earlier.

"That river was there before us all and will be there long after we're all gone, Cathal. It's been good to the people who live near it," Granda observed.

Cathal couldn't help but think that there was some strange business happening on that same river nowadays, his mind pre-occupied with the mission that lay before him in the early hours of the morning.

CHAPTER SIX

At 10pm, Cathal went to bed and, not long after, he heard Granda lock up downstairs and retire to his own bedroom. He didn't sleep, though. Before he got under the covers, he changed into the darkest clothes he owned - a black tracksuit pants and a black hooded top. On his wrist was his sports watch. His black wellington boots were hidden under his bed with his schoolbag, which would double as his rucksack. He put the new torch and a pair of black gloves in the bag.

Cathal planned to be in position in a hiding place at Ballycastle Pier by 3am, as it was shortly after this time that he had seen the light and the boat on the two previous nights. It would take him about a half an hour to make it on foot to the pier so he would have to be leaving the house at 2.30am at the very latest. He lay in bed, nervous and excited, all the while wondering if he was crazy to be even considering such an audacious expedition.

Despite his excitement, he worried about accidentally falling asleep but prepared for that eventuality by keeping his mobile phone (which hadn't had reception since he arrived in Ballycastle) in his pocket on vibration alert, setting the alarm clock for 2.20am. It was just as well that he did because, despite his anticipation, Cathal drifted into a light slumber, with the mobile phone serving its purpose by waking him at exactly 2.20am without any noise that would wake Granda.

When he woke, his heart was pounding. He thought that he had overslept, however, he soon realised that he was still on schedule. Ever so quietly, he pulled back the duvet, got up and retrieved his wellingtons from under the bed. Repositioning the duvet, Cathal tried to heap it in the middle to give the impression of a sleeping figure underneath, just in case Granda checked in on him while he was out. He placed a balled-up black T-shirt on the pillow, semi-concealed by the duvet, in an effort to replicate the shape of his head.

Carefully opening and closing his bedroom door, with his rucksack on his back and carrying his wellingtons in his hands, Cathal crept slowly downstairs. He dared not breathe as he passed Granda's door at the foot of the stairs and it was reassuring to hear the old man snoring loudly as he went by.

After going through the living room and kitchen, he was at the back door. Turning the key, Cathal thought for one last time about the insanity of what he was doing. He hesitated briefly at the door before deciding, once and for all, that he was going to find out what was going on down by the river. He put his wellingtons and gloves on, opened the door and stepped outside.

"This is it," he thought, "it's now or never."

The night was cold and breezy and the moonlight occasionally faded behind clouds as Cathal hurried along towards Ballycastle Pier. When the moonlight was unobstructed, a dark shadow accompanied him on his way, but, shadow or no shadow, the boy felt very much alone, more alone than ever before in his life. The bare branches of the swaying trees rattled in the breeze overhead and, occasionally, a dog could be faintly heard barking somewhere in the night air.

The constant flowing of a mountain stream was audible in the distance, growing louder as Cathal drew nearer. As he crossed the small bridge that spanned it, the energy of the spring water racing downwards to the sea made him feel full of life. He thought of the thousands of people who had travelled that road before him over the centuries and wondered if their ghosts were still making the same journey. He hoped not, and then convinced himself that even a ghost would want its head examined to be out at that hour of the night.

Cathal met nobody on his journey to the pier and arrived there at 2.59am, a minute ahead of schedule. If he had encountered a car or any other vehicle, at the first sight of headlights in the distance his plan was to hide in the nearest gateway or opening. Thankfully for Cathal, the situation never arose. Approaching the pier, he carefully looked all around to make sure that the coast was clear, so to speak.

Ballycastle Pier was located at the end of a long and narrow country road, flanked on either side by dense woodland, known locally as Coill na Marbh Woods, literally translated as the 'woods of the dead'. There was no house or any other building around for at least a kilometre and there was no lighting in the vicinity of the pier. The pier jutted out into the water, perpendicular to the grassy anti-flooding embankments that ran alongside the river. To the side of the pier was a concrete slipway for launching and landing small vessels.

Cathal found himself a comfortable position hidden behind the top of the embankment, a short distance west of the pier. From there, he would be able to see any activity that might ensue at Ballycastle Pier or across the river at Killcrown Pier, which was about one hundred metres away. All he had to do now was wait and not be seen.

All the while, since leaving Granda's cottage, Cathal had been active, moving along the road as discreetly and as quickly as he could, his mind occupied by the task of reaching the pier, adrenalin running through his veins. Now that he was stationary and effectively on stakeout, the full madness of what he was doing finally registered in his brain.

"Oh my God! Here I am, staking out a river bank, on my own, at three o'clock in the morning in late November. For what? To satisfy my curiosity?" he asked himself.

It was then that Cathal began to feel afraid. He suddenly regretted what he was doing. He was betraying Granda's trust and potentially putting himself in danger's way. He thought about the sort of crazy people that might be involved in some sort of illegal activity that he might now be dangerously close to. He thought about Seánín Solas and what might happen if he really did exist. He wondered what he would do if he saw a light near the pier or a boat in the water. Up until now, he hadn't really thought that far ahead.

"It's time to abort mission and return to base. This is the most stupid and irresponsible thing that I've ever done!" he told himself.

He looked in all directions to make sure that there was nobody around before emerging from his vantage point. Looking at his watch, with its faint light, he saw that it was just gone 3.10am. Still looking all around, as he walked the short few paces along the top of the embankment towards the pier, something on the opposite side of the river at Killcrown Pier caught his eye. He instantly threw himself to the ground and gently slid his way back into a concealed position behind the top of the embankment.

From there he watched, aided by the moonlight, as two people moved a small boat onto the slipway beside the pier. One of the people appeared to tie the boat to the slipway and both walked away, disappearing out of view again. A few minutes later, both reappeared, walking towards the boat, but, this time, each was dragging something in their wake. They came to a stop at the slipway and, after a few moments, lifted whatever they were dragging into the boat.

In total, four items were loaded aboard. Whatever it was didn't seem too heavy, as both were able to lift the items by themselves, although they looked large and bulky. After untying the rope again, each figure stood into what little space was left in the boat. They both bent down and picked up oars from the floor of the boat, which they used to launch themselves away from the slipway and paddle towards Ballycastle Pier.

Cathal could see the boat coming closer and closer, as the pair rowed across the near-still waters of the river. He shivered with dread, his heart racing, as the boat reached the slipway on the Ballycastle side of the river, just metres away from where he had taken up his new hiding position.

Cathal was certain that this was the boat that he had seen from his bedroom window the previous night. He wanted to run away, such was his fear at that very moment, but it was too late for that now, as any attempt to move would surely give away his position and that was not something that he was willing to risk.

He constantly monitored his immediate surroundings for fear of anyone else being around but, so far, it seemed like it was just him and the two people in the boat. When the boat came to a halt on the slipway, both occupants jumped out and pulled it further up the concrete slope. There, they began to unload their cargo and it became clear to Cathal what it was - trees!

The trees measured about two metres each, in Cathal's estimation. Just as he realised what the cargo was, Cathal also realised who the boatmen were. In the moonlight, he could distinctively make out a tall, slender figure and a short, heavyset figure. However, he was only fully sure of their identities when he heard one of them say, "Okay, we can hide the boat again now, Barty".

Cathal was watching his two new best friends and was flabbergasted. He wondered what Billy and Barty were doing and why they were doing it. The Shanahans dragged the boat, oars inside, up the concrete slope and into a cluster of trees about ten metres from the slipway, where they proceeded to cover it with a large sheet of black polythene followed by some sizable branches of evergreen trees.

Then they returned to the trees, which they had left at the top of the slipway. They took two trees each and placed them side by side, with the trunks facing away from the water. Each boy got to work tying a short length of rope to the trunks of their respective trees. They then used the ropes to drag the trees along the ground behind them.

When they reached the embankment at the top of the slipway, they started to walk eastward, away from where Cathal had been positioned. The smooth grass surface made it easy for the boys to pull the trees along and, within a few minutes, they had gone a considerable distance from the pier and slipway.

Cathal had to decide whether he would follow or not and, eventually, curiosity again getting the better of him, he decided to pursue them at a distance, being extremely cautious not to be seen in the intermittent moonlight. He looked at his watch, which read 3.35am. He still had plenty of time before he would have to return home.

Cathal carefully picked his steps along the embankment, staying as far behind the brothers as he could while still keeping them in his sight. After about two hundred metres, the brothers turned ninety degrees to the left, sliding down off of the embankment and onto a pathway that led north and away from the river bank into the woods. The boys continued on this pathway for a further three hundred metres, going deep into the woods to where they came to another steep embankment which ran in an east-west direction.

Cathal watched from afar as the boys struggled to climb the embankment with the trees, but manage it they did, eventually. Once on top, they turned right in an eastward direction and moved along a grassy surface again, with more dense woodland lying to their left, beyond the embankment.

When the boys were about thirty metres ahead, Cathal attempted to scale the embankment himself. He was almost at the top when he lost his footing and slipped, causing him to slide back down to the bottom and land on a dead and dried-out branch of a furze bush, which snapped loudly under his body weight.

The brothers stopped immediately, certain that they had heard a noise to their rear. There was an audible and brief discussion between the pair as they scanned the moonlit path that they had just travelled, with Cathal remaining totally motionless and silent, lying face down against the side of the embankment. Almost certain that he had blown his cover, he was afraid to move and stayed in the same position for as long as he could. All the while, lying there on the damp grass, he expected to be discovered but, somehow, he wasn't seen.

Eventually, when he was confident that it was safe to move on, he got to his feet and made a fresh attempt to scale the embankment, taking extra care with his footing on this occasion. When he got to the top, he could barely make out the two figures moving far off in the distance to the east, about one hundred metres ahead. He had lost a lot of time lying against the embankment and would have to quicken his pace to keep up with the Shanahans.

Cathal moved briskly along, picking his steps carefully in the moonlight. Sometimes, at places where the trees closed in overhead, it got very dark and he had to proceed much more slowly and carefully, with his torch being of no use to him in such a covert pursuit. After one lengthy stretch of overhead trees, Cathal lost sight of the boys briefly before speeding up and glimpsing them again.

Suddenly, the whole countryside went dark when a large, thick cloud moved in front of the moon. This cloud didn't go swiftly past like the others, though, and it was also carrying rain, lots of rain. A few heavy raindrops quickly became a torrential downpour. He could no longer see any trace of the Shanahans and, before long, Cathal was all alone in the middle of the 'woods of the dead' in the pouring rain.

By now, he was an emotional wreck. He was very afraid and extremely nervous, constantly looking over his shoulder. Every sound he heard caused his heart to jump as he became paranoid about what might be in the woods. He reached for the torch in his rucksack and kept it in his hand, ready to power it on if needed but still reluctant to use it in case the Shanahans would see it from whatever far-off position they were in.

Cathal was also very angry with himself that he had been so stupid to leave his warm, cosy bed and go out into the cold, dark, creepy, and now very wet, woods. Thoughts of his grandfather's stories of ghosts and the supernatural filled his head once more. The way he looked at it, he had two choices. One was to turn back and retrace his steps and the other was to keep going along the embankment, which seemed to be leading him to nowhere. His gut instinct was telling him to turn around.

He also figured that it had to be getting very late and a quick glance at his watch told him that it was 4.23am. He calculated in his mind that he could be back in his bed for just after 5.30am if he turned around now. However, Cathal was a stubborn young man and he was determined to find out where the Shanahans had taken those trees and what they were planning to do with them. He made a decision. He settled on continuing along the path for a further ten minutes and, if he hadn't discovered anything more enlightening by then, he would turn back and still manage to be home for 6am.

The rain continued to bucket down and Cathal was soaked from head to toe. His wellingtons had partially filled with rainwater and they made a squishing sound with every step he took. The embankment just seemed to go on forever, as he quickened his pace to a slow jog, aware that, at any point along the way, the Shanahans might have left the embankment and he might have gone past their turnoff point.

He stopped briefly to catch his breath and check the time. It was 4.30am, just three more minutes to the turn-around time. He proceeded further, moving a little faster now, knowing that he was nearing the end of his exploration for the night. The rain lightened and flashes of moonlight began to break through again.

Another look at his watch told him it was 4.32am. One more minute and it would be time to turn back. Moving along, he thought he could see a dark shadow on the embankment up ahead in the distance. As he moved closer, the clouds cleared from in front of the moon and the countryside was lit up again. It looked as if the embankment ran straight into the side of a steep rock cliff face.

It was 4.33am, the designated turn-around time. Cathal knew that he had promised himself that he would turn for home, but now that he was so close to the end of the embankment, he decided that continuing would be reasonable.

He wondered if there was a pathway along the base of the cliff face. Very soon, it became clear to Cathal what the embankment was, what the cliff face was and that there would be no path leading away from it but, rather, one going straight through it. In front of him, Cathal could see the dark, horseshoe shape of a large tunnel. The embankment that he had travelled along was the old dismantled Ballycastle stage of the Great Southern Railway line.

⁓

STANDING ALONE IN THE MIDDLE of the night at the entrance to this great tunnel, Cathal believed that very few people would ever have found themselves in the same scenario. The breeze whistled through the tunnel, creating a haunting and eerie sound, and Cathal thought that it sounded as if a steam train was approaching in the distance.

He listened for any voices that he might hear, but there were none. If Billy and Barty were in there, he would surely have heard them, given the indiscreet acoustics of the tunnel. Stepping one pace inside the mouth of the tunnel, Cathal looked for the moonlight through the opening at the far end, but there was no end in sight.

"Enough is enough. If I'm going in here, I'll be using my torch," he resolved.

He flicked on his torch and bravely stepped deeper into the tunnel which was just large enough for one train at a time to pass through and which was lined all around by beautiful stone archways. A steady volume of water dripped from the roof into puddles on the tunnel floor, the sound of water on water echoing throughout.

About twenty metres in from the opening, Cathal's torch light detected a large stationary object. After initially getting a fright, he moved closer to inspect and soon saw that it was, in fact, a tree leaning against the wall of the tunnel, the trunk resting in a puddle of water underneath. It wasn't any ordinary tree either but a beautiful green spruce tree, the type commonly used as Christmas trees. Further investigation revealed that there were no less than twenty-eight trees in the tunnel.

"This must be a stockpile of trees that the Shanahans have put together," Cathal thought, and an explanation for their behaviour finally dawned on him.

"They have started a little business of their own, cutting down Christmas trees, which surely don't belong to them, with the intention of selling them on. The tunnel is their storage depot until it's time to move them on as Christmas gets closer."

This, he figured, was something they were doing every night for at least a week, given that there were twenty-eight trees in the tunnel and they seemed to have the capacity to cut four every night.

"No wonder they've been oversleeping in the morning and falling asleep in class," Cathal thought. "No wonder Barty has a bad cold and Billy's been buying batteries and rope at the shop. It's not just orchard apples that these lads are interested in getting their hands on."

Suddenly, remembering the time pressure that he was under, Cathal checked his watch. He got a dreadful shock when he saw that it was 4.47am. He was late, very late. He started back along the route that he had just travelled. He calculated that it would be well after 6.15am by the time he would get home and, with Granda usually waking at 7am, this was far too close for comfort.

He wondered where the Shanahans had gone after dropping the Christmas trees in the tunnel. There surely was a more direct route back home from the tunnel but Cathal didn't have the luxury of time to try to find out, because, if he took a wrong turn or got lost, he might not make it back on time and Granda would find him out.

He ran most of the way home, making it into the yard at 6.17am. Quietly and carefully he took off his wellingtons, socks and gloves at the back door, taking them in his hands before going in, locking the door and creeping past Granda's bedroom door and up the stairs. He figured that his bare feet would leave less of a water trail on the linoleum floor than his socks would.

Ever so relieved to be back in his bedroom, he quietly hid his wet clothes and bag under his bed and dried his wet skin and hair with a towel before getting under the duvet at 6.28am.

"What a night!" Cathal thought as he drifted off to sleep, deciding that, later that day, he would confront the Shanahans about their little enterprise.

∼

IT WAS AS IF HE HAD not slept at all. It was more like he had blinked his eyes and it was suddenly time to get up. Granda was standing over Cathal at the side of his bed, shaking him and telling him to hurry up and get dressed or he would be late for school. Granda had already opened the curtains and when Cathal came to his senses, he realised that it was 8.40am.

He had slept through his alarm clock, the sound of which had brought Granda into his room, a dangerous development given the activities of the preceding hours, although Cathal had all of his tracks well covered, with no obvious clues lying around.

Like a zombie, Cathal made his way downstairs, hoping that Granda would not take notice of his wet schoolbag - which he didn't. Two hours of sleep was simply not enough for Cathal and he was exhausted as he left for school, taking only a slice of toast in his hand as breakfast. At 8.50am, the Shanahans showed up as planned, both looking as exhausted as Cathal.

There was very little conversation between the trio on the trip to school, as they trudged along the road, each one more tired than the other. Cathal had envisaged having some fun trying to coax a confession from the Shanahans regarding their capers but now he was in no such humour and said nothing about the events of the earlier hours.

∼

BY THE TIME GRANDA had all of his salmon and turf sold, the grand total of all of his sales came to €7,600. This was €900 short of his repayment target and, with nothing else of any great value available to sell, Granda started to worry. The thought of the thugs coming back and what they might do to him, or Cathal, gave Granda a sick feeling in his stomach. He was determined to go to Dublin and make the full repayment well in advance of the December 8th deadline.

He didn't want to give those brutes any further excuse to set foot on his property or interfere with him in any way. He regretted ever having gone to that source to borrow the money that he needed but that was done and there was nothing that he could do to change it. All he could do, he thought, was bring the whole frightening episode to a speedy conclusion.

"I'll have to go to my emergency, emergency fund," Granda concluded. "It's the only way that I'll make up the total amount in time to keep them away from here."

He looked at the clock. It was just gone 1pm. He would have to work quickly if he wanted to have his money retrieved before Cathal returned from school. He made his way to the foot of the stairs and the secret compartment under the first step. Lifting the lid, Granda took out the folded sheet of paper that lay within. Replacing the step, he sat down on the bottom one and unfolded the sheet of A4 paper.

"Ah, yes, this is my treasure map alright," he thought. Although he hadn't looked at it for a few years, he instantly recognised the map that he had drawn to help him remember where he had stashed away the €1,000 in €50 notes that he had won on a horse called 'Silver Jaro' on the last day of Cheltenham in 2008. The horse romped home at 50-1 and Granda had put €20 of his pension money on it. It was a nice win and, rather than spend it, he thought it would be prudent to keep it for a rainy day. "Well, it's pouring cats and dogs now," thought Granda, as he rose to his feet, put on his wellingtons and made for the sheds to fetch his spade.

The map consisted of a diagram showing the cottage and farm sheds, the 'Mountain Field', a sycamore tree, a holly tree and a spot marked by an X, in true treasure map tradition. With spade in hand, he marched to the old iron gate that led from the farmyard to the 'Mountain Field', a piece of land about the size of a football pitch, which was perfectly rectangular and sloped gently towards the hill.

Even though it was located on high ground and ran along by the foot of the mountain, the 'Mountain Field' would be rich with green grass in the summer months and, even now, in the middle of winter, maintained a thick cover of short but lush grass. At the north-west corner of the field was a large sycamore tree. This was the starting point of reference on the map and Granda quickly made his way towards the tree from where he followed the written instructions: 'Starting from the sycamore tree at the NW corner, take twenty large paces eastward, keeping along by the northern ditch. After twenty paces, you should be in line with a holly tree.'

Granda looked over his left shoulder and there was the holly tree, standing beautifully on the northern ditch, heavily laden with bright red berries, which contrasted spectacularly with its dark green leaves. He read the final lines: 'At the holly tree, head straight south for twenty large paces. This will bring you to X. Dig for two feet to retrieve your winnings.'

Granda took a ninety degree turn to his right and duly started pacing his way towards the point marked X. Counting the paces aloud as he went, he developed a sudden sense of panic as he reached the high teens. There, a few paces before him, he could see the earth had been disturbed at point X.

Without continuing the count to twenty, Granda rushed to the disturbed ground, which indicated that a hole had been dug and filled in again.

He frantically dug with his spade, which wasn't very difficult, given that the sod was soft, having only recently been turned. After a few seconds of digging, he felt his spade strike a metal object. Pulling the object out of the ground, he could see that it was the same butter cookie tin that he had buried in 2008, although very rusty now. Fearfully removing the lid, Granda was disgusted to see nothing but a rusty interior, with his €1,000 fund gone.

"Who on earth would have found this?" he wondered. "It was never the lads cutting the silage in the summer time. They'd never find it and, anyway, the sod was fully intact for the last few years and nobody would have known that anything was buried there. It couldn't have been someone with a metal detector. The chances of anyone finding something that small in such a big field are so slim and they'd hardly have been in here for long enough without me seeing them."

Granda thought that it must have been someone who got their hands on the map and, by the appearance of the disturbed soil, it was quite recently. He went through the possible suspects in his head. The only people that had been inside in his house recently were himself, Cathal, Peggy Moore and the public health nurse. He knew that he hadn't taken the money himself and whatever he thought of Peggy Moore, she certainly wasn't a thief. That left only the nurse, who was never out of Granda's sight, and Cathal.

"Surely my only grandson would never have done this to me?" he thought.

Then he remembered everything that Peggy Moore had said about him falling in with the wrong company and the potential bad influence of the Shanahan brothers. Granda tried to dismiss his suspicions as premature and unfounded, but the more he thought about it, the more plausible it seemed.

He thought about how Cathal had been at home all by himself from 3pm on Monday afternoon and would have had ample time to search his cottage from top the bottom, find the map, retrieve the cash and put the map back in its hiding place. He painfully concluded there and then that Cathal was the prime suspect and that he would ever so subtly attempt to verify his suspicions.

Granda replaced the soil exactly as he had found it. He went back to the house and, after putting his spade back in the shed and putting the map back in its hiding place under the step, he lit the fire in the living room using some spare pieces of wood that were left over from the builders' recent renovations. He then began to prepare a meal to share with Cathal on his return from school.

∼

ALL THREE OF THE BOYS struggled hard not to be overcome by their tiredness all day, with Barty falling asleep in class again, earning a fourth detention in a row. Cathal earned two hundred lines for not being able to recite 'Ancient River Clane', having known it by heart the previous night. Billy allowed the Master to walk all over him all day, with insult after patronising insult going without rebuttal, his mind too tired to function in any defensive way.

During lunch break, Cathal and Billy stood around with their hands in their pockets making idle talk, as if conserving what little energy they had left. At the end of the school day, the three boys unanimously decided to skip their routine visit to the shop, going straight home instead. Along the way, having found a burst of energy and mischief from somewhere within, Cathal decided it was time to start asking questions.

"You two seemed very tired today - is everything okay lads?"

"Yeah, fine. I'm not tired. Sure you're not tired, Billy, are you?"

"No, I'm not tired."

"What makes you ask that, Cathal?" asked Barty.

"Well, it's just that I thought that both of you looked very sleepy this morning."

"Well, yeah, I mean, we always look sleepy in the morning," answered Billy defensively.

"Yes, but it seemed to be more visible today for some reason. Then, of course, there was Barty, falling asleep in the classroom, again."

"I was up late watching a DVD," answered Barty.

"What DVD was that?"

"Ah, it was, ah, I forget the name of it now."

"*Back to the Future*," interrupted Billy. "And I was watching it too, so no wonder we'd be tired."

"Oh, I love *Back to the Future*," replied Cathal enthusiastically. "Was it *Part I, II* or *III* ye watched?"

"*I*," said Billy while, simultaneously, Barty said, "*II*".

Then, trying to amend their collective mistake but

creating a deeper mess, Billy said "*II*" and Barty said "*I*".

"Maybe it was *III* ye watched," said Cathal sarcastically with a smile.

"No, it was definitely *II*, said Barty. "It was the one where Michael J Fox went back in time."

"Doesn't he go back in time in all of them?" asked Cathal, privately enjoying the situation that his questioning had created.

"No, I think he goes into the future in one of them."

"Which one was that Barty?"

"I don't know, I can't remember. It's so long since I've seen any of them."

Billy poked Barty with his elbow to shut him up but it was too late and the admission had been made.

"But I thought you watched one of them last night?" quizzed Cathal, by now trying hard not to laugh.

"So, what type of movies do you like, Cathal?" asked Billy, blatantly ignoring Cathal's prying.

"Well, lots of types really. I really liked *Castaway*, where Tom Hanks is out in his little boat in the water. *The Railway Children* is another one of my favourites, especially the bits with the tunnels. Christmas movies, anything with a Christmas tree, that sort of thing."

Billy and Barty glanced at each other, neither of them knowing what to say, both continuing their walk towards home. Cathal, knowing that he had touched a few nerves, decided to push further.

"There was this great movie that I saw one time about these two brothers who sneak into a forest in the middle of the night and cut down some Christmas trees and make their getaway by boat and hide the Christmas trees in a disused old railway tunnel."

Billy and Barty stopped walking. Cathal, now knowing for sure that they knew that he knew, kept walking and, as he did, spoke over his shoulder to the Shanahan brothers.

"Why so are ye stopping? Is it something I said?" he asked as he came to a halt, grinning from ear to ear.

"How on earth did you find out?" asked Billy seriously, worry etched on his face.

Then, turning to Barty, he asked, "Did you open your big mouth?"

"I said nothing," insisted Barty.

"Find out what?" replied Cathal, playfully maintaining his innocent demeanour.

"Look at your face, you couldn't fake to save your life. You know what I'm talking about."

Then, sarcastically, "Oh, is it about the Christmas trees and the boat and the railway tunnel? Ah sure, that was obvious."

"Obvious. How was it obvious?" blurted Billy.

"Well, it was a combination of all the evidence really," said Cathal, as he proceeded to inform the Shanahans about how he had come to discover their escapades, beginning with how he had seen the light, then the boat and concluding with the discovery of the tunnel.

"Hold on a minute. What light did you see?" asked Billy.

Cathal explained in detail what he had seen from his bedroom window on Monday night.

"We don't carry a light. It's too dangerous. We'd be seen for certain," said Barty.

"Yeah, sure, pull the other one why don't you, Barty," said Cathal. "Sure, how could you see what you're doing without lights?"

"He's not joking," asserted Billy, "we don't carry a light or a torch or anything like that. After a while, your eyes adjust to see enough in the dark."

"But, I even saw you getting the batteries for it at the shop," insisted Cathal.

"Batteries? Ah, yeah. They were for my alarm clock."

"Well, if it wasn't ye with the light, who was it?"

"Maybe it was Seánín Solas," exclaimed Barty.

"There's no such thing or being as Seánín Solas, you fool," dismissed Billy.

"There is, you know," said Barty assuredly, "our Dad told me about him."

Billy, not wanting that line of conversation to go any further, or to compromise Barty's memory of his father, turned the questioning on Cathal again, as the trio once more began to move slowly towards home.

"So, all the time last night, you were following us through the woods? That's just creepy, man."

"Yep. From the slipway, all the way, nearly as far as the tunnel. I almost gave myself away climbing up the railway embankment when I slid onto a furze bush."

"I knew I heard something," gasped Barty. "I heard a snap and we stopped but we couldn't see anything. I was sure it was Seánín Solas. That's a relief."

"Yeah, that was me."

The boys laughed and Billy and Barty felt a slight blow to their pride for having failed to conduct their affairs in secret.

On the remainder of the journey home, Billy gave Cathal a full account of events to date. He told of how he had met two men outside the shop one evening after school, about a month earlier. It turned out that they were the men who were doing the renovation works at Granda's house.

They started talking about work and how scarce construction jobs were, when one of them said that they sold Christmas trees every year in the weeks before Christmas to help make a living. Billy, instantly spotting an opportunity, told them that he could supply them with Christmas trees for €40 each. After some haggling, they settled on a price of €25 per tree.

The men asked no questions about where the trees would be coming from and, even if they did, Billy wouldn't have told them. Billy pledged that he would have at least sixty trees, maybe more, for them by December 8th. One of the men gave him a mobile number and said to phone as the time approached to arrange a rendezvous point and payment for the trees.

"We've been out most nights with the last two weeks. One night, the fog was so thick that we lost our way and hit a rock and we both ended up in the water. Not a nice experience. All along, we were able to bring only two trees per night but since our R&D department, i.e. me, thought of using the rope to pull them along, we can bring four per night now. Last night was our first night doing that."

"It was a good idea," Cathal remarked.

"Yep, one of my better ones," smiled Billy. "You know, we'd really boost our profits if we could carry six per night."

"Whoa! Hold on a minute," exclaimed Cathal. "You're not seriously suggesting that I get involved in this?"

"Well, it's up to you," said Billy persuasively. All I'm saying is that we'd enjoy the company and it would be worth €15 to you for every tree that you carry yourself."

"Hey - that's not fair. You're only giving me a tenner per tree," objected Barty.

"That's because you slow me down. So, what do you say, Cathal? Are you in?"

"Hold on a minute, guys. I mean, isn't this stealing? Those trees belong to someone else. They aren't yours to cut in the first place," Cathal reasoned.

"Oh my God, Billy, he's going to tell on us."

"For God's sake, Barty, I'm not going to tell on you, I'm just saying."

"Shut up, Barty, and leave this to me. Look, Cathal, I know that at first sight this looks a bit dodgy, but think about it, man. It's like Peggy Moore and those apples - these trees are just sitting there in a dark, wet and cold forest, doing nothing, while all the time they could be bringing happiness to people in sitting rooms all over the county.

"The Murphys are loaded to the gills and will never miss the trees. It's a victimless crime. In fact, I wouldn't even call it a crime. It's a victimless action. But, more than that, it's actually going to make people happy. The people who buy them will have beautiful Christmas trees. The two builders will have money to buy presents for their families for Christmas and, last but not least, we'll have a few euro to put towards our education."

"Put towards our education? That's a good one," interrupted Barty.

"Shut up, Barty. So, Cathal, what do you say?"

"I don't know guys. This is very risky business. I mean, it's a lot of hassle and effort for €15 a tree."

"It may not sound like much now but if you can carry two trees per night every night between now and December 8th, that would be €30 per night for ten nights, that's €300. Not bad."

Cathal's gut was telling him to run a million miles but the lure of the money was extremely hard to resist. He wasn't thinking of his own pocket but that Granda could surely do with the help, especially as he seemed to be having trouble paying back his debts to some very nasty people. He would also have been lying if he said that the invitation didn't excite him somewhat. The whole thing seemed to be a great adventure. As they reached the little bohereen leading to Granda's cottage, Cathal gave his verdict.

"I'm in."

"Yes! I knew you were sound from the start," Billy exclaimed, slapping Cathal's back.

"Welcome to the Company," added Barty, extending a formal handshake to Cathal.

"So, when do I start?" asked Cathal, in keeping with the theme.

"Meet you right here tonight at 2.30am sharp," said Billy. "You know what to wear and all that. I'll bring rope for you. No need for a mobile phone, no reception anywhere around here. Don't be late and get some sleep in the meantime."

"I will, I do, I will," answered Cathal. "See ye then guys."

The boys went their separate ways. Cathal was full of excitement; he had never been part of anything like this before and was relishing the adventure that lay ahead. Granda had a lovely big plate of bangers and mash waiting on the table for Cathal when he got through the door.

As the pair tucked into their meal, Granda began to probe.

"So, Cathal, how're you doing for money at the moment? Do you still have the €20 that I gave you the other day?"

"Well, Granda, I spent a few euro at the shop but I still have most of it."

"Oh, I see. Well, let me know if you need any more."

"I will, Granda."

"By the way, Cathal, I'll have to take you up to show you the 'Mountain Field' one of these days. Have you ever been up there? It's the one right behind my farm sheds."

"That'd be nice, Granda. I've never been up there."

"Are you sure you weren't up there?"

"Ah, yeah. I'm sure I'd remember that."

Granda wasn't quite sure what to make of Cathal's answers. He thought that either he was a good liar or innocent.

"Are you fairly familiar with where everything is in the house at this stage, Cathal? You know where everything is kept and hidden?"

"Yeah, more or less. Granda. Is it okay if I go and lie down for a while, I'm not feeling too well."

"Sure, Cathal, off you go."

Cathal, who in reality was exhausted and needed some sleep, quickly disappeared upstairs to his room, but Granda's suspicions had been roused further.

"Did he just make that up about not feeling well to

get himself out of a sticky situation?" Granda wondered. "What if he is a thief? How can I have him living under my own roof?"

A short while after Cathal had gone to his room, Granda crept upstairs and into the locked room. He checked his cigar box for his money and counted it twice. It was all there. Nobody had interfered with his money yet and he wasn't willing to take any chance. He took the large bundle of notes out of the cigar box and carefully placed it in the inside pocket of his jacket. He would be keeping it close to himself from now on, just in case.

Cathal slept until 8pm that evening. Even then, it was Granda checking up on him that woke him. Cathal got up and did his homework, including the two hundred lines that he had picked up from the Master. At around 11pm, he went back to bed to 'sleep'. At exactly 2.15am, he got out of bed and, once again, embarked on a journey into the night.

CHAPTER SEVEN

The Shanahan brothers were waiting for Cathal when he arrived at the bottom of the bohereen at 2.30am exactly. From there, the three boys quickly made their way to Ballycastle Pier, at one stage having to hide in a gateway for about thirty seconds, as a solitary motor car passed on the road. They arrived at the pier just before 2.55am. On their approach, they carefully surveyed the area, still conscious of the unsolved mystery of the light that Cathal had seen.

When all seemed normal, the boys proceeded to uncover the rowing boat and dragged it down to the slipway, where they launched it without delay, arriving at the Killcrown side of the river in a matter of minutes. Pulling the boat up the slipway at Killcrown Pier, the boys quickly made off for Murphy's Woods, which were less than a hundred metres from the pier.

A breach in the perimeter fence allowed for easy access. Just inside the entry point, Billy picked up a handsaw that he had hidden beneath some leaves. From there, the boys went a few metres into the woods to where a vast plantation of Christmas trees had been set some years earlier. As soon as he was gone deep enough into the plantation so that missing trees would not be noticed from the road, Billy identified six suitable trees and started sawing them down while Cathal and Barty brought them back to the little boat, one by one.

In less than half an hour the three boys were back on the water, rowing towards Ballycastle, their little boat loaded to absolute capacity and sitting quite deep in the water. They swiftly unloaded their cargo upon reaching land and concealed their boat as before. With ropes attached, each boy dragged two trees in his wake as far as the tunnel, bringing to thirty-four the total number of trees in storage. To Cathal, the journey from the slipway to the tunnel seemed infinitely shorter that night than on the previous night, even though he was dragging a heavy load.

The boys quietly joked and laughed along the way and each enjoyed every minute of it. After depositing the trees in the tunnel, Barty and Billy led Cathal through to the exit on the other side. From there, a short walk along the dismantled line brought them to a gate on the side of a bohereen that led all the way back to the road within a few hundred metres of the bohereen to Granda's cottage. The boys parted at their usual place and Cathal was back in his bed just before 5am.

"What an efficient piece of work," he thought to himself as he drifted into sleep.

~

EVERY NIGHT, THE NUMBER of Christmas trees in the old railway tunnel increased by six, as the three boys regimentally kept with the routine that they had established. Overall, the operation advanced very smoothly. The weather stayed reasonably good for the time of year and all of the nights, bar one, were dry, calm and mild. A few showers of rain on one night made the task a little unpleasant but it was nothing compared to the rain that fell on the night when Cathal had followed the Shanahans into the woods.

The trees all remained very fresh despite some having been cut for a few weeks. The coldness and darkness of the tunnel made for ideal storage conditions and the puddles on the tunnel floor provided an excellent irrigation system.

The mysterious light that Cathal had seen from his window had not reappeared and, ultimately, the boys agreed that it must have been a farmer out looking for some lost sheep, or that there was some other innocent explanation. Still, although not admitting it to the Shanahans, Cathal could not get the thought of Seánín Solas out of his head and was constantly nervous whenever he was in the woods.

With a buffer zone of trees strategically left standing, nobody from Murphy's Estate ever seemed to notice the sizable area of felled trees that had developed over the weeks, and the boys concluded that nobody must walk that part of the plantation in the winter time. The water was always calm for the river crossing and the boat and oars were always left undisturbed at the place where they were concealed.

On one night, Cathal was very lucky not to wake Granda when one of his wellington boots slipped out of his hand whilst coming down the stairs. It made a hollow thud, but, luckily for Cathal, Granda kept snoring.

Night after night of irregular sleeping patterns took their toll on the boys, though, and, in particular, their schoolwork suffered, with Barty frequently falling asleep in class and Billy and Cathal often having to fight hard not to commit the same offence. Cathal found that his concentration levels and information retention capacity had dropped considerably and, for the first time in his life, he was struggling slightly with his academic work. He reassured himself that, once the trees were handed over on December 8th, it would all be over and everything would go back to normal, allowing him time to catch up at school.

On the home front, Billy and Barty's mother didn't suspect a thing. Preoccupied with looking after her younger children and working two jobs to keep bread on the table, Mrs Shanahan allowed her two eldest boys more freedom than most boys of their age, and she trusted them to be responsible. The boys had a pact to place money in an envelope and drop it through their mother's letter box some day after getting paid for the trees.

They both knew how hard their mother worked and how scarce money was and wanted to help her out in any way that they could. Even after a donation of €100, Barty would still have €240 for his own use. Billy would have a total of €1,560 from which he would contribute €500, leaving him with over €1,000, a lot of money for a thirteen-year-old. Cathal also planned to give all of his €300 to Granda, in the same way that the Shanahans planned to anonymously surprise their mother.

Granda was still none the wiser about Cathal's nocturnal activities. After the loss of the €1,000, he had been suspicious of Cathal and had planted a number of traps around the house to see if the boy would prove whether or not he was dishonest. Granda would casually leave a bundle of €20 notes on the mantelpiece or the dining table if he was leaving the room or going to the farmyard. Cathal would have plenty of time to help himself to a share of it. Of course, the money would have been carefully counted in advance by Granda, with the noughts in the serial numbers filled in with a blue marker, just for proof of the origin of the note in the event of a confrontation.

The money was always left untouched, though. One day, Granda inadvertently dropped a €5 note on the floor in the kitchen and Cathal later picked it up and gave it back to him. All of this changed Granda's initial suspicions regarding his grandson's involvement in the disappearance of the 'emergency, emergency fund' but it still did not answer the question of what had really happened to it.

By Saturday, December 7th, Granda was very worried. He had less than twenty-four hours left to pay back the €8,500 that he owed but he was still €1,000 short. He would have been only €900 short had he not lost €100 on a horse the previous day, in a vain effort to raise €1,000. He couldn't go to Dublin to the loan shark without the full amount, so he braced himself for another visit of the thugs to his cottage, during which he planned to hand over the €7,500 and promise the remaining €1,000 with further interest by Christmas. He hoped that this would suffice, but something inside him said that it would not be enough for the people he was dealing with.

Saturday, December 7th, was also a significant date for Cathal and the Shanahans. That night would mark their final trip to Murphy's Woods and, by dawn, they planned to have all of their trees shifted and their money collected. All three boys used the Saturday morning off school to catch up on some valuable sleeping time, with Cathal staying in bed until midday and the Shanahans not surfacing until early afternoon.

As soon as he woke, Billy made a phone call to the builder that he had met at the shop and the rendezvous point was agreed. The man agreed that he and his partner would bring two vans with large trailers to the gate on the bohereen near the railway tunnel at 4.30am sharp, where the boys would be waiting with eighty-eight trees. An overall figure of €2,200 was agreed and Billy was delighted that everything was set for the transaction to proceed.

As usual, at 2.30am, the three boys met at their regular meeting point. They proceeded towards Ballycastle Pier, taking extra caution not to be seen, it being a Saturday night when more traffic would be on the road. Arriving at the pier, everything was peaceful and they proceeded to cross the river to Murphy's Woods to cut their last six trees. As Billy was leaving the woods with the final tree, he brought his handsaw with him, rather than leaving it under the leaves as he had always done.

With the boat loaded up, the boys set sail across the River Clane for the last time with a sense of euphoria that they were on the final leg of a long, hard journey. When they were at the midway point in the water, Cathal, who was sitting at the front of the boat, called out to the Shanahans.

"Stop rowing, lads, get down. There's someone at the pier in Ballycastle."

Through complacency and carelessness, brought about by the occasion of the final night's work, the boys had failed to notice the van and trailer that had parked at Ballycastle Pier while they were in Murphy's Woods. All the lights were turned off but it was still just about visible. They stopped in the water and looked as closely as they could.

"I think there's someone standing at the end of the pier," whispered Barty.

"Yeah, I can see him too," whispered Cathal, "he's looking straight at us."

"Guys, I think I've figured out what's going on here," whispered Billy. "I bet that's the builder and he's after getting his wires crossed. He's not supposed to meet us here but, sure, who else would it be?"

"I don't know, Billy, why would he come here if he's not supposed to meet us for another hour at a different place?" whispered Cathal.

"He probably wanted to get here early and I bet he took the wrong turnoff," insisted Billy, "look, trust me on this one, lads."

Before there was any time for further discussion, Billy was standing up in the boat again and calling aloud to the man on the pier.

"Ahoy there!"

"Ahoy!" returned the voice.

"That's him alright," said Billy to the boys. "Come on, Barty, row."

The boys began rowing towards the slipway once again and, as they did, the man moved back from the pier and down the concrete slope to where he could meet the boat as it came ashore.

As the boys were getting out of the boat at the bottom of the slipway, the man began walking towards them. As he came closer, a second man appeared from behind the van and began walking towards the boys too. Billy suddenly realised that these weren't the builders that he had met at the shop. Just as suddenly, Cathal realised who they really were.

∼

S%%INCE COMING TO BALLYCASTLE%%, just under two weeks earlier, Cathal had the image of two huge, bearded men constantly etched in his mind as a result of the incident in Granda's backyard. Therefore, there was no mistaking the identity of the men at the slipway as soon as they became distinguishable.

"Oh God, lads, we're in trouble here," Cathal spontaneously blurted as soon as it dawned on him that the two men waiting were the same thugs.

"Yous are bleedin' right, yous are in trouble," said one of them, while the other grabbed Cathal and Barty by the collars of their coats.

Billy immediately made a drive for the man holding his brother and friend, swinging a wild punch at his huge frame, at which the brute only laughed before his accomplice grabbed Billy in an armlock. Barty tried to break free of the grip of the man holding him but, again, his efforts were useless and both men just laughed at the attempt.

"Now boys," the man holding Billy calmly said, "listen to me and listen very carefully. If you make any more attempts to be physical with us, we're goin' to hurt yous really badly. Understand? Yous boys are after creating a big headache for us, so don't push us any further, or we might do something very serious."

The thugs marched the boys past the large horse trailer to the side of the van, where they tied their hands behind their backs with plastic cable ties. They tied them so tightly around their wrists that the blood could scarcely circulate in their hands. That done, they searched them for mobile phones, which none of the boys were carrying due to the lack of coverage.

Then, bundling the boys into the back of the van, the thugs tied each of their ankles together. Sitting them upright and back to back in the middle of the floor, they proceeded to tie all three of them together, using a rope that they wrapped tightly around their chests. Finally, one of the men got a roll of thick grey tape and wrapped it around each boy's head, ensuring that their mouths were covered, allowing them to breathe only through their noses.

"Now shut up or if I have to come back to yous, yous will end up in the water."

Bang! The side door of the van slammed closed. The three boys sat in the dark, terrified and unable to communicate properly. Billy tried to shuffle his way free but, as he did, his efforts caused the rope to cut into Cathal and Barty's ribs, who, through their moans, forced Billy to stop.

Meanwhile, they could hear the sound of their boat being dragged all the way up the slipway and beyond where the van was parked. After that, there was a prolonged period of silence.

"What could the thugs possibly want with us?" Cathal thought. "Surely this has nothing to do with the money Granda owes? It seems that they didn't recognise me from the last time. And, surely, they don't want anything to do with a few miserable Christmas trees?"

He racked his brain trying to figure out why the thugs would be waiting there for them and then thought that maybe the builders had some dispute with them, but all of the possibilities didn't seem to add up. Then he thought about the light that he had seen and wondered if it was anything to do with that.

After some time, the boys thought that they heard the sound of an engine coming closer and getting louder. They all privately concluded that it was a boat engine approaching on the river from the direction of the harbour. They heard it come to a halt at the pier, after which voices could be heard. Within seconds, they could hear the sound of items being loaded into the horse trailer.

Whatever the items were, they seemed heavy, as there was quite a lot of grunting and dragging along the floor of the trailer and a solid bump when the items were dropped into place, causing the van to spring slightly. For about ten minutes, the trailer was loaded up with cargo from the boat until it left the pier and headed away back towards the harbour and the sea. Within minutes, another engine, slightly different to the first one, could be heard approaching from the harbour side.

The boat pulled up at the pier and the offloading of cargo began again. After about five minutes, the boat pulled away and the door of the trailer was slammed shut and bolted. The side door of the van slid open for a moment, long enough for one of the thugs to look in to see that all three boys were as they had been left. The door slammed closed again and the engine of the van started and was driven away from the pier, pulling the trailer behind it.

By now it was 4.30am and thoughts of not being on time to liaise with the buyers of the Christmas trees were far from the boys' minds as they worried frantically about where they would be taken to. Over the sound of the engine, they could hear the muffled voices of the thugs in the van. After a few minutes, it came to a halt. It sounded like the thugs were arguing, as their voices grew louder and sharper.

The van moved on again, so quickly that the three boys almost tipped over. More arguing ensued before the van came to an abrupt halt again. After further bitter arguing, the boys felt the van reversing and turning around. Soon it was on the move again and then it slowed, as if taking a sharp corner. The ride became much rougher all of a sudden and the boys could feel that they were going up a steep hill. In the back of Cathal's mind, he knew that they were climbing the narrow bohereen up the hill to Granda's cottage.

~

Granda was asleep when a mighty racket woke him. Before he knew what was going on, one of the thugs had rushed into his bedroom, turned on the lights and pulled the petrified old man out of his bed. Through the open bedroom door, he could see that his front door had been kicked in and now the man in his room was demanding that he would "get dressed and hand over the money".

Granda put on the clothes that were resting over the back of the chair beside his bed, including his jacket, in which he carried the €7,500 wad of cash and the key for the locked room upstairs. As soon as he was dressed, the thug marched him into the living room and sat him down on a chair. His accomplice then came through the front door, into the living room and pulled a chair into the middle of the floor, opposite Granda, where he sat down.

"Now old timer, before we go any further, who else is in the house?"

"Nobody else," said Granda, frightened and not wanting to bring Cathal into it, "it's just me. I know why you're here and I have your money for you."

"Are yous sure there's nobody else?" asked the man again, this time in a more menacing tone.

"No, I swear it's just me," assured Granda, praying that Cathal had heard the commotion and had hidden somewhere upstairs.

"Take a look anyway," the man on the chair instructed the other.

While the other man was searching the house, Granda produced the money from his pocket, accidentally pulling the key out too, which fell to the floor.

"What's the key for?" asked the thug on the chair, swiping the wad of notes out of Granda's hand.

"That's the key to one of the rooms upstairs where I used to keep some of my valued items but I sold them all to help pay back my debt to you."

"Harry, come here," called the thug, picking the key off the floor.

The other thug returned to the room.

"Check out the rooms upstairs."

He took the key and thundered up the stairs. At the top, he went to the left and opened the door of Cathal's room, which wasn't locked. After a few seconds, Granda could hear the sound of items being flung to the floor and knocked about as the thug searched the room.

"It's only a matter of time before they find him," Granda thought, but, to his amazement, after about a minute, he heard the footsteps moving towards the room with the locked door, which he entered using the key and proceeded to thrash also.

The old man wondered where his grandson could be hiding. Meanwhile, the man sitting opposite Granda had come to realise that there was €1,000 less than agreed in the wad of notes.

"There's money missing from here, old man."

"There's €7,500 there. That's every last penny I have right now. I'll have the other thousand and interest by Christmas, I swear."

"That's not the way we operate, old man."

"But I was robbed of €1,000. I'd have had it for ye weeks ago only for that."

"I really don't care what happened. Anyway, yous are another loose end that needs to be tied up."

"What do you mean 'loose end'?"

"Ah, it doesn't matter. It won't bother yous."

Granda grew pale with the sound of those words.

"Nothing," the other thug shouted from upstairs.

"Alright, on your feet," the man in the living room ordered, grabbing Granda under the armpit and dragging him to his feet, marching him upstairs and into the room opposite Cathal's bedroom, which was now an awful mess, with shelves broken and cabinets overturned.

"Get the others, Harry," said the man holding Granda, "and something to tie this fella too."

A few minutes later, Harry reappeared, this time marching Cathal and the Shanahan brothers up the stairs to the room where Granda was. The cable ties around their ankles had been cut but their hands were still tied and their mouths covered. The rope had been retied and now kept them together like a chain gang.

"Cathal! Don't hurt him whatever ye do," Granda shouted with concern when he saw his grandson coming up the stairs.

"Will yous ever shut up," shouted the man holding Granda, before taking the roll of tape from his accomplice and swiftly rendering Granda speechless with a tight wrapping.

The brutish duo then proceeded to cable tie Granda's hands and ankles, as well as reapplying the ties to the three boys' ankles and then tying all four together in the middle of the floor. As they worked, the man who had been questioning Granda spoke.

"Little did we know when we came down to this backwater a few weeks ago that it would be such a rewarding trip for us. Fair enough, yous came up a bit short with the repayments, old man, but what an ideal location for an importing business. It was just unfortunate that these three fools showed up at the wrong time.

"After all me work, walkin' the entire coast one night, checkin' for potential problems. We'd be halfway back to Dublin by now. Do yous know, old man, we wouldn't have even called back to yous were it not for these three seein' us. The boss even told us to leave yous be and get out of here clean but we couldn't take the chance of lettin' the rats go free. I didn't want to drown 'em, even though Harry would have.

"I don't do kids and pensioners so I thought, let's bring 'em here and everyone will be taken care of. We'll get to keep a few grand for ourselves and we'll have a nice quiet place to hide everyone and nobody will die. I'm sure by the time they find yous, we'll be well and truly gone."

Granda and the boys were relieved to hear that they weren't going to die. Each of them privately feared that this was the end. Inside, Cathal was furious with himself for bringing this trouble on Granda. The Shanahans, similarly, felt terrible for involving Cathal and his grandfather in the whole saga.

"Alright. They're not going anywhere," said Harry, having finished tying the rope tightly around all four.

"Pleasure doing business, old man," said the other, before turning off the light and locking the door, leaving the four detainees bound and gagged on the floor in the dark.

They heard the lights being switched off downstairs before the front door was pulled shut and the van doors were closed. The engine started and the van turned in the farmyard before taking off at speed back down the narrow bohereen. All four listened to the vehicle being driven away and contemplated a long, uncomfortable wait until someone would find them.

Then, as if it was a dream, the sound of a Garda siren shattered the near silence of the Ballycastle countryside.

EPILOGUE

It was Monday and Granda had just finished a beautiful late breakfast in bed when he picked up *The Kerry News* and read the headline once again - 'Local Heroine Blows Cocaine Landing'. Then, reaching for the *Irish Express*, he chuckled as he read the headline and subheading, 'It Pays to Have a Nosey Neighbour - Freed hostage pays tribute to 999 caller'.

"Billy Shanahan couldn't resist the temptation," Granda thought, laughing heartily.

Under the headline was a huge image of Peggy Moore, her hair curled and face all made up, holding a telephone to her ear in a staged photo, with the caption, 'Peggy Moore, recreating the moment she called the Gardaí when she became suspicious of nighttime visitors to her neighbour's home'.

Ballycastle was swarming with reporters from all parts of the country and even the world, with four international news services having correspondents in the village. Business was booming for Ted Hanratty and McCarthy's Bar was transformed into a temporary media centre.

Lying on top of his bed, in a white fluffy bathrobe and soft white slippers, Granda switched on the television, just in time to see Paul Sheehan from TV Ireland standing on the roadside, broadcasting live for the *Lunchtime News*, with Granda's little cottage in the background.

"Well, Paul, what can you tell us about the latest developments in the Ballycastle drugs seizure?" asked the newsreader in the studio.

"Well, John, Gardaí have now confirmed that this is, in fact, the largest seizure of illegal drugs in the history of the Irish State. In the early hours of Sunday morning, over two tonnes of pure cocaine, with an estimated street value of €700 million, was brought ashore at a pier just a short distance away from this isolated cottage behind me.

"Three local schoolchildren, who discovered the plot, were unable to alert the authorities before being captured by the drug smugglers and brought here to the cottage, where they were tied up and held, along with the grandfather of one of the boys, from whom a quantity of cash was stolen but which has since been recovered.

"When the smugglers arrived at the cottage, a concerned neighbour, named locally as Peggy Moore, alerted Gardaí to the unusual events and, as they made their getaway, they were intercepted by the local Garda, Jim O'Sullivan. The smugglers fled through the fields but were apprehended a short time later by a team of back-up Gardaí and a Garda K-9 unit.

"The two men were charged at a special sitting of the Circuit Court in Tralee this morning on numerous drugs-related charges and arrests in Dublin have led to a high-profile criminal, based in the north inner city, being charged with similar offences at a sitting in Dublin in the last hour.

"In another incident, two men were arrested on Sunday morning close to the scene of the drugs haul, having been found in possession of eighty-two Christmas trees which were stolen from a nearby plantation. The men were charged with the offence at the same sitting of Tralee Circuit Court this morning, where one of the men then bizarrely confessed to having stolen €1,000 a few weeks earlier off the same man who had been tied up by the drug smugglers. He said that he took the money when he was working in the elderly man's house but insisted that he had nothing to do with the drugs haul.

"Gardaí are still trying to figure out the significance of six further Christmas trees, which were found in a boat beside the pier where the drugs were brought ashore. The good news from this episode is that the rightful owner of the trees has now donated them all to charity, so that they will be used in homes for the festive season ahead.

"Gardaí and forensic experts are still carrying out a technical examination of the scene and, for now, the elderly man and the children involved are said to be recovering at a local hotel.

"Paul Sheehan, *Lunchtime News,* TV Ireland, Ballycastle, County Kerry."

Granda switched off the TV again and reached for the phone beside his bed, thinking that a couple of questions remained unanswered. He dialled 0 for reception and asked to be put through to Cathal Kavanagh's room. Cathal answered.

"Cathal, I think you have some explaining to do."

"Yeah, we'd better meet for lunch, Granda, this could take a while."

"Meet me in the lobby in five minutes, Cathal, I've got all day."

"I'll be there Granda, but you might need all night too! See you shortly."

Cathal hung up the phone, glad that Granda didn't sound too mad but he knew that he and the Shanahan brothers would receive punishment for what they had done and he hoped that it would not be too severe. They had stolen and that was wrong and there would have to be consequences.

He went to the window of his hotel room. Outside, two of the hotel staff were almost finished decorating a Christmas tree on the front lawn of the hotel. He thought how splendid the decorated tree looked, far happier looking than the trees that he and the Shanahans had left in the railway tunnel.

"I suppose the difference is that this tree has a home," he thought. "That changes everything."

Their decorating task finally completed, the proud staff switched on the lights of the tree for the first time. Cathal gazed in awe at the multitude of bright colours that twinkled and sparkled in the grey December afternoon. In his mind he was looking forward to getting back home to Granda's cottage to start decorating their own tree. He thought about the future and his new home in Ballycastle and something told him that many more adventures with the Shanahan brothers lay ahead.